GWEN-HOPE THIS IS A WONDERFUL
READ.
LOVE

The HIDDEN ARROW
of
MAETHER

The Hidden Arrow of Maether

of

AIDEN BEAVERSON

DELACORTE PRESS

Published by Delacorte Press
an imprint of Random House Children's Books
a division of Random House, Inc.
1540 Broadway
New York, New York 10036

Visit us on the Web! www.randomhouse.com/kids
Educators and librarians, for a variety of teaching tools,
visit us at www.randomhouse.com/teachers

Library of Congress Cataloging-in-Publication Data

Beaverson, Aiden.
The hidden arrow of Maether / Aiden Beaverson.
p. cm.
Summary: When she runs away from her cruel stepfather rather than be married off to a follower of the evil
Rane, Linn begins to discover her own special gift and
wonder if she might be one of the lysefolk, followers of
the Great One about whom she has only read.
ISBN 0-385-32750-1
[1. Fantasy.]   I. Title.

PZ7.B38059 Hi 2000
[Fic]—dc21
                                                      00-026105

The text of this book is set in 13.5-point Centaur.
Book design by Debora Smith
Manufactured in the United States of America
November 2000
10 9 8 7 6 5 4 3 2 1
BVG

*Dedicated with all my love to
Laura,
Michael,
and most of all Bob.
You are my treasure and my life.
Without you, Bob, this book
would have remained hidden.
Thank you.*

I extend heartfelt affection and gratitude to Guy Thorvaldsen and Yvette LaPierre for their friendship, encouragement, and commitment to this book. You're the best!

———

*M*any thanks to Robin McKinley Dickinson and Garth Nix for their invaluable advice, and to Wendy Loggia and Jill Grinberg for their expertise, long-suffering, and help. I appreciate you.

He has made a Hidden Arrow
and fletched it for His will, not mine.
He will hide it in His quiver
until the ripened time.
And in that day the Arrow flies
to foil my will and crime,
attend this Hidden Arrow;
in a hand shall dwell the sign.
—The Farsight of Rane

One

"Take the path, Linnet! Take the path!"

Linn jerked awake, instinctively clutching the worn leather-bound book that lay on her chest, her breath pounding out in short, quick bursts. Long tendrils of dark hair clung to her damp face and neck. She groaned and sat up, swinging her legs over the side of her bedstead and burying her face in her hands. The dream had come last night—again.

It always started the same way. As soon as she fell asleep, a tornado of emotion snatched her up in a dizzying whirl. Then Farr's voice pushed through the dream-storm, rising and falling in an unintelligible stream of sound, tantalizing her with just one clear word here and another there. "Linnet! . . . I . . . Great One . . . always . . . Rane . . . flee!"

And then the dream-storm tossed her down, down, down until she landed, swaying and trembling, atop a towering needle of stone. It felt so real. . . . Sweat ran down her face now as she remembered the dream-wind cuffing her, yanking hairs from her plait, teasing her with the little shoves that threatened to push her off the pinnacle. And then, from across a deep chasm, her father appeared, alive and well. His urgent voice exploded in her ears, almost deafening her, shouting out the phrase that had awakened her once again that morning—

Whump! The worn curtain that separated Linn's loft room from her stepbrother Carey's space swayed in the breeze of his wake. Too impatient to take the steps one at a time, Carey had jumped from the middle of the loft ladder to the floor below on his way to mornmeal.

"Girl! Get down here if you want a bite before you take the goats out to pasture!"

Linn cringed as her stepfather's hard voice surged up the ladder. Shuffling over to the basin, she splashed her face with water and plaited her waist-length hair. She squirmed into her undershift and tugged on her scratchy goathair overshift.

Then, as she did each morning, Linn plucked the worn leather book from where it lay on her mattress, rubbing her cheek against its cover. Her father's old Lysetome, filled with the wisdom of the Great One. Farr had gotten it from his father, and his father from his father.

Linn's great-great-grandsire had seen the first uprising of the Ranites in Maether, the first attack against the Truens. He'd fled the island of Col to come to Laefe, where he hoped his family would be safe. To ensure their safety, Great-great-grandfarr had hidden the Lysetome away and taught his children to worship the Great One in secret.

But the worship of the demon Rane had spread, stamping out the Truens wherever it went. Within a generation, the Truens had waned almost out of existence. Now only a few remained, hiding their allegiance from their neighbors. If their beliefs were discovered, the Truens found themselves ostracized or attacked and stripped of all their possessions. Sometimes they were killed.

Not everyone in Maether worshipped Rane. In fact, most held halfhearted allegiances to minor household deities that hadn't enough power to keep a hearth fire lit. But these ordinary people lived in fear of the Ranites, of their violence, and of the tyrannical demon they worshipped. Who knew what Rane might do, when the Ranites might attack an innocent man or woman? Even now, Linn sometimes heard of the Ranites calling up the demon, torching far-off villages because they refused to welcome Ranite leadership. Was it any wonder that most people tried to placate the Ranites and avoid conflict?

Farr had taught Linn to keep her Truen faith and her counsel. The Lysetome had become her own rare jewel, one she'd managed to conceal since she'd first found it on her eighth birthday, hidden beneath her bedclothes. Her mother must have put it there. It was the only gesture Mam had ever made that told Linn she remembered her first husband. At first, Linn had kept the sacred book under her thin mattress, even during the day. But now that she was older she wanted it close to her heart and safe from her Ranite stepfather's prying eyes.

Tucking the Lysetome inside her shift, Linn followed the scent of baking bread down the ladder. Carey was already seated with the other children at the long plank table. His dark head bobbed up and down as he shoveled in boiled oats and fruit as fast as he could. As usual, he ignored Linn with a scorn he'd absorbed from his father. Mam scurried around the room, checking the bread baking in the wall oven and filling up plates and cups as fast as they were emptied. She scowled at her daughter.

"Why can't you get up on time, girl?" Mam clucked angrily, shooting a nervous look at her husband, seated at the head of the table. "Now get to your place and look to your brothers and sister!"

Linn bent her head, her eyes fixed on the rush-strewn floor. Although her tongue burned with an angry retort, she bit her lip and seated herself quietly at the end of the table next to her youngest half brother and as far away from Domm, her stepfather, as possible. As soon as she sat down, three-season-old Peri grabbed her shift with a jam-covered hand and looked up at her with meltingly blue eyes.

"Rinna." He lisped her name in his baby voice. "Rinna. I show you somefing." He held up a speckled brown egg. Peri had recently been given the task of hunting out the chickens' eggs each morning, and this was his first find.

Linn smiled down at his dark head. "Good work, Peri! Where did you find it? In the stedyard?"

Peri nodded. With a look of immense satisfaction, he rewarded himself by slopping more jam on his hunk of bread.

Mam crouched on the bench next to Domm and scowled again. Domm didn't like conversation at mealtime. So Linn plopped a gluey mound of boiled oats into Jenna's bowl. The six-season-old hadn't yet plaited her flyaway hair, and it formed soft little curls around her face. *Blurp.* A scoop for Bran next. With a sly glance at Linn, he slid a sticky wooden spoon off the table and began to smear jam on the ends of Jenna's hair.

"Stop it, Bran!" Jenna squealed, and pushed the jammy spoon away. "Now look—you made me spill the milk!"

Heaving a sigh, Linn reached over Peri to mop up the mess. She rubbed the jam out of Jenna's hair with a flannel, then swiped it at Bran's face.

"Nyah! Missed me!" Bran stuck out his tongue.

Linn pointed at the chair next to Carey. "Sit over there, Bran. Jenna, you come here by me." Then she plopped down, sighed again, and sawed a piece of bread from the new-made loaf, spreading it with fresh white curds.

Domm grunted. "So you finally decided to join us, eh?"

Linn stopped midbite as her stomach churned. Here it came, another bout of ridicule from Domm. She carefully placed the bread back on her plate, knowing that her stomach would soon be a hard ball of sickness. She didn't want to throw up again. *Why can't he just let me eat in peace? Just once!*

"Enjoy your late lie-ins while you may, girl. It won't be long before wifely duties force you up before dawn."

Linn's head jerked. "What wifely duties?"

Domm cocked one eyebrow and made a rude hand gesture. "Whichever wifely duties Tykk assigns you. Last night, after the Ranite meeting, I promised you to him."

"Y-you *what?*" Her eyes flew to her mother. Mam lowered her head and hunched a shoulder. Linn's heart squeezed tight in her chest.

"You heard me, girl." Her stepfather's low forehead wrinkled in irritation. "I've made a betrothal for you. A good one with Tykk." Domm waved the knife he'd been using to cut his cheese. "So get used to the idea."

Linn tasted salt on her dry lips. All girls on Laefe

were betrothed when they came of age. But—but it seemed so soon. And a betrothal to Tykk? She cast another look of agony at her mother. Mam kept her head turned away, making a small, careful business of helping baby Fen as he sucked on a crust of bread.

"Mam?" Linn pleaded, suppressing the sob that rose in her throat. "Mam? Did you know about this?"

"Just obey your father, girl. He knows what's best." Mam wouldn't meet her daughter's eyes. Then, with a flustered movement, she picked up Fen and left the room, shooing Peri, Bran, and Jenna before her.

"You're lucky, you know, girl." Domm leaned back in his chair, belched, and hooked his fingers in the belt that hung low beneath his paunch. "I could have betrothed you before now. Young Seth wanted you—he asked me several times." Gooseflesh pimpled Linn's skin at the thought. "But I still needed you to herd goats when he asked last year. So I put him off, and he went after Bera—got her too."

Carey moved closer to Domm. He was older than the other children—almost thirteen seasons—and the product of Domm's first marriage. He took great pleasure in lording it over Linn, since he held favored status as Domm's firstborn. Now he snickered into his mug of goat's milk. "He got her all right, Fa! I saw her last week—bruises all over her arms and a belly out to here." He stretched his arms in a wide circle. Linn closed her eyes and swallowed.

Domm's eyes narrowed as he grinned. "But now, girl, you're almost fifteen seasons. Ripe enough for a wedding, eh, boy?" He clapped Carey's back and the boy smirked. "And Carey's old enough now to herd the goats himself, isn't that right, son?" Carey's smile slipped from his face, and his mouth fell open.

"But wh-why Tykk?" Linn stammered. "He's a Ranite—wouldn't he rather wed a Ranite woman than me?"

Domm's look was hard and pointed. "Laefe has girls far comelier than you. You're as skinny as a girl three seasons younger! And with no dowry—you'd be lucky to get the youngest son of a poor farmer! But Tykk would have you. He likes those black eyes of yours." Domm's upper lip lifted in a sneer.

A ball of bile rose into Linn's throat. She swallowed the evil-tasting lump with difficulty.

Domm rested one heavy forearm on the table and pointed a thick finger at Linn. "And anyway, what makes you think he'll not get a Ranite woman?"

It took a minute for the implication of Domm's question to sink in. "Y-you mean you're going to force me to become Ranite, even if I don't want to?" Linn's voice shook as she wrapped her arms over the Lysetome hidden beneath her shift. How could she turn her back on the Great One and abandon the only thing she had left of Farr? She'd submitted quietly to all Domm's other demands. But he couldn't take away this last thing and enslave her to Rane—could he?

"I serve Rane. Most of the men on Laefe serve Rane. My children will serve Rane once they're fourteen seasons. I wed your mother when you were five with the understanding that she would not become Ranite. After all, she was well dowered. Else I'd hardly have looked at her twice—a widow saddled with another man's brat! But the dowry paid for this sted. Because of that, I agreed that she'd never have to become a Ranite. But there was no agreement about *you*. Tykk wants you, and wants you Ranite, so Ranite you will be." Domm stabbed another hunk of milky cheese with his knife for emphasis. His tattoo, the red circle of Rane, mocked Linn from his forehead.

A vein pulsed in Linn's neck, marking the silence. Domm didn't know that she and her mother came from a Truen home. He never would have wed Mam otherwise, and it was shameful for a widow of childbearing age to remain unmarried. But now, after all these years of secret worship, to suggest that Linn would not live her life as a Truen but as a Ranite slave—it was too much. A surge of panic coursed through her, loosening her tongue.

"But I can't become a Ranite! Rane's nothing more than a liar and deceiver, a puffed-up demon who takes on human shape when it suits his plans. What has Rane ever done but twist and destroy the good things the Great One created? My *real* father would have died before he saw me serve Rane!"

Domm looked over at his stepdaughter, his jaw grinding away at a chunk of apple. "What's this talk of the Great One, eh, girl? Are you a secret Truen?" A grin flitted across his fleshy face as he swallowed. "Well, Truen or not, you just prophesied your own future. Your father's dead, and now you'll serve Rane."

A buzzing began somewhere in Linn's head. Her body suddenly felt light, and far, far away, as though she looked down on it from somewhere in the rafters. In shock, she heard herself choke out, "I *won't* be Ranite! And I won't wed Tykk!" before jumping to her feet and racing out the sted door.

Her stepfather, although short and heavy, reacted swiftly. He pounded into the stedyard after her, switch at the ready. His large, meaty hand laid hold of Linn's upper arm, jerking her off balance. She landed flat on her back, all the breath knocked out of her. Helpless, she stared up into her stepfather's beefy red face. His tattoo blazed wetly through the sweat on his forehead. She smelled the smoked meat he'd eaten at mornmeal as his breath huffed from his panting mouth.

Domm's expression as he motioned for Linn to get up made her hands tremble. "Just what made you think you could escape?" He shook his head, smiling to himself. "All these years, all the beatings I've given you, and you haven't learned yet? You'll do what *I* say, be who *I* say you are. Understand?"

Linn rose from the dust on quivering legs. A drop of cold perspiration inched down her face. She stared with dread and fascination at the switch in his hand.

"Well, girl?" he demanded again, his eyes becoming flat disks carved from icy blue stone.

"No," Linn whimpered. Two people seemed to inhabit her body. One cowered fearfully before Domm's switch, and the other chided her for fearing him. *Stand up to him! Have some pride!* Linn longed to do as the second urged, but the first had control.

"All right, girl." Domm spoke harshly, poking her with the slender tip of the switch and enjoying her involuntary jerk. He liked being in control, liked the fear that oozed from her. "I guess there's just one way to convince you." He spun her around and forced her to bend over.

"Lift the back of your shift, now, girl. We'll make it three this time. One on the hindquarters for trying to run." The switch whistled out and stung across Linn's seat, leaving a thin trail of blood on her undergarment. "And one on each leg for your disrespect to Rane and for mentioning the Great One in my sted." The whine of the switch sliced through the air; then the switch itself cut into the flesh on the backs of her thighs.

Linn bit her lower lip until it bled, each slash of the switch bringing forth an unwilling yelp. Her hands and knees ground into the dust as the last blow forced her down, sweating and retching with pain.

"Now, get going. You can herd the goats without a midmeal today, to teach you obedience." Domm looked down at her, his face a hard, controlled mask. He'd relished every second of inflicting the pain, just as any Ranite would. But he wouldn't show his gratification. His detachment added to Linn's terror, and he knew it.

Linn hunched over her knees and wrapped her arms around her body. She hugged the book hidden beneath her shift. Her own father's Lysetome. Her *own* father— not Domm. A blast of defiance steamed through her. "No!" she spat out. "I won't obey you anymore! I won't herd the goats; I won't wed Tykk! And no! I won't become Ranite!"

Domm raised his thick eyebrows so that they almost touched his tattoo. "No?" he asked, almost laughing. "*No?* That's a word I must teach you not to use to me— or any man!" His switch snapped back and whistled toward Linn's face. Instinctively her right hand jerked up, palm spread wide.

The switch split the skin of her palm in two. For a moment, she felt no pain. She stared at her gashed hand in disbelief, amazed that it hadn't been her head. Her eyes met Domm's, and he shrugged.

"You're lucky this time, girl," he said. "I meant to hit that sullen face of yours. Even though that might have made Tykk unhappy." He caught the thin end of the switch in his left hand. "But goats still need to eat, whether you're bleeding or not. So get to it!" Then he turned toward the sted, not bothering to look back and see if his stepdaughter obeyed him.

Two

Linn stumbled up from the dirt, cradling her throbbing hand against her chest. Fresh blood filled her mouth, and her shift stuck to the blood that trickled down her legs. Unwilling tears obscured her sight, but not enough to hide Domm as he swaggered back to mornmeal and his passive wife.

She turned and limped toward the far side of the goat pen, the side that wasn't visible from the sted. At the foot of a solitary young tree she huddled, rocking back and forth.

"Oh, Farr, Farr, why did you have to be the one to die? Why did Mam have to marry Domm? Why does he hate me? Why did you leave me all alone?"

She cried out all the despair and loneliness she'd been holding inside, cried until her mouth clotted with spittle. She sagged against the tree, limp as the crust the baby had been chewing at mornmeal. The thought of her mother, Fen on one hip, scurrying from the table, made her grind her teeth. Something inside her snapped, a husk crushed beneath an unbearable weight.

Mam! Why don't you protect me? Why do you let him do this to me? I loved you—I imitated you! I try to please him, try to keep out of his way and obey his rules! I try so hard! But no more— never again! Go ahead—let him beat you! But he'll never touch me again! I hate you as much as I hate—

A flicker of movement on the hill halted her rush of emotion. Linn froze. *What is that?* A long, silky trail of bent grasses and weeds appeared, winding its way through the tall plants on the hillside. But these grasses lay flat, as though blown by a strong, steady wind. Linn licked her left forefinger and held it up. The wind was coming from the north, no mistake. Yet these grasses bowed to the east. Why? And *how?*

Wincing as her wounds stretched open, she eased herself up, using the tree at her back as leverage. Something flexible and rough flicked her face. She started and stared, just in time to see the branches of the little sapling reach down and touch her face. *They touched her face!*

"Get off!" Linn twitched away, backing up against the goat pen to gawk. The tree bent low, bowing the way with a lordly gesture. And, like the grasses, it pointed east, away from the sted.

East. Linn stepped forward a few feet, and the flattened grasses rolled out even farther. She looked behind her. The tree had righted itself and once more blew with the north wind.

She pivoted back to the hill. The grasses still lay there, beckoning her. She wet her lips with the tip of her tongue. "Wh-what is this?" A path. A path—*the* path? Of her dream? Surely it was a sign, maybe even . . . No, no. She shook her head. But the question wriggled back. Could this be a lysegift, a blessing bestowed on Maether by the Great One?

Linn pulled out the Lysetome and ran her finger down the list of lysegifts. Mapping, healing, speaking with animals, weaving . . . There was no path-gift listed. But what if it was something special? Something sent to save her from the fate Domm had planned? "Is it?" she breathed.

A tingling in Linn's midsection, above her last rib, distracted her. She scratched at it. "Oof!" An explosion took over her chest. A cluster of gossamer-thin yet tough-as-iron threads tugged at her gut. And they drew her in the same direction as the path. Up into Laefe's central hills.

She placed her hands across her ribs and looked down, half expecting to see something attached to her skin. Nothing. But the threads continued to urge her on, and the path to beckon. She'd yearned to run away so many times before but had never given in—until now. "Why not?" she asked aloud. "Who cares about the goats, anyway? Or Domm—or Tykk!" She began to run, recklessly letting the pulling threads draw her along the unfolding path.

She panted after the grassy trail on and off for hours, dipping through valleys and winding around fir-scented tree trunks, chasing the path into the hills that towered over the island's deep harbor. Then it vanished. The plants blew with the north wind. Linn turned in a full circle. Nothing.

Her breath whistled in and out over cracked lips. Her wounded hand began to throb and burn. She needed water, *now*. Laefe's hills were full of little brooks and streams, and it didn't take Linn long to find one. She plunged her face into it and drank her fill. Then she washed her gashes. "Ow!" The deep one on her hand broke open. She wrapped it with a torn-off piece of her undershift, then drank again and replaited her hair.

Making for the tallest tree she could find—an evergreen—Linn picked her way up its narrow trunk. Although the branches swayed dangerously under her weight, she made it almost to the tree's crown. From her perch, she saw the water of Laefe's harbor wink far off in the sunlight. The tide was coming in.

The rush of rebellious freedom ebbed away, and the thought of Domm's switch returned. She ran a finger over the makeshift dressing on her wounded palm. What would Domm do to her if she went back to the sted now? *I'd be lucky if I could even walk after he got through with me!* No, there was no returning. Even starvation was preferable.

She situated herself more comfortably in the tree. Would the path appear again? Could it help her escape? But to where? Laefe was a small island, too small to hide her from Domm for long. Somehow, he would find her and force her to wed Tykk and perhaps even force her to worship Rane.

Linn sighed and put her head down on her knees, letting her mind wander. *If only, if only I really, truly had a lysegift.* If only she could find the legendary City of Trees, where the lysefolk lived, and use her gift as they used theirs, releasing the good skill of it into Maether. It had been a long time since she'd bothered to pray to the Great One, but now her lips moved against her rough shift on their own.

"You made this world. You made Maether so beautiful, Great One. Why can't you change my life? Are you there? Are you listening to me? Farr taught me to call on your name—and now I do!"

Silence. "Ha." Linn gave a croaky little laugh. A wry grin twisted her mouth, and she shrugged. *What did you expect? To hear a voice from the sky tell you you're a lyse? You're alone—better get used to it.* But deep inside her nestled a wisp of comfort. Gradually she relaxed as the tree branches rocked in the wind. "At least I'm safe from Domm for now," she murmured drowsily.

The sun had already thrown a red glow into the western sky by the time Linn struggled awake. She stretched her cramped body carefully, rubbing her stiff limbs. The wrapping on her hand was a mass of clotted blood. She examined it in the rays of the setting sun. Fresh blood oozed from beneath the barely formed scab. Unable to resist, she picked at it while her thoughts returned to her dilemma.

Domm won't just leave me alone in the hills. He's promised me to Tykk. How can I escape? Farr's parents were dead, so she couldn't run to them. Even here in Laefe's hills, she wouldn't stay hidden for long. Domm would find her and punish her. "And I'll be right back where I started," she concluded, resting her forehead on her bent knees.

The sea breeze struck her legs, and she shivered. The temperature was dropping quickly as the sun set. She stared at the clouds massing in the dark sky above her while, half aware, she continued to pick at her wound. The clouds were the immense, threatening mountains that warned of an early fall storm. They piled up and up in a tall pyramid, their edges blazing orange and red with the light from the setting sun. The formation resembled a sail.

"A giant ship to take me away," Linn murmured. Suddenly the tugging sensation was back with a vengeance, pulling so hard she lost her balance and smashed her wounded palm against rough bark trying to steady herself. The imperious little threads urged her toward the harbor. And, as her eyes followed their lead, Linn saw something that made her realize why they pulled so insistently.

"A ship! Of course!" She gulped as she caught sight of a bobbing vessel tied to the harbor dock. "I'll stow away!"

Three

As the massing clouds promised, an island storm soon broke. Overhead, branches mimicked Domm's arm, thrashing wildly up and down in the wind. Lightning shot across the sky, glaring down on the landscape below, while thunder echoed every flash. Then rain began to fall in opaque sheets.

After her initial drenching, Linn gave up trying to keep dry. It was impossible. The rain wasn't just falling; it drove down, digging shallow divots in the soil. Linn squinted and shielded her eyes with her hand, trying to peer through the impenetrable layers of darkness and rain, but she could only see a couple of feet ahead. If the strange path she'd seen earlier had reappeared, it was invisible in the deluge.

"I hope I make it to the harbor without falling over a cliff," she muttered as she shuffled along. For some reason, goathair cloth always felt rougher when wet. It chafed against the wounds on her legs, rubbing them even rawer than before.

"Yipe!" Linn scrambled for a foothold but fell backward into thick, running mud. "The harbor path!" She shook her muck-covered hands, and mud flew into her face. With a grimace, she regained her footing and followed the mud flow cautiously, her head snapping toward the slightest sound. Cobbles pushed into her bare feet. She'd made it into the village.

The rain faded to a drizzle. Below, in the harbor, the ship dipped, tugging on the ropes that tied it to the dock. Thank the Great One that Laefe's steep cliffs meant the ship was able to harbor there instead of dropping anchor further out. Suddenly a light appeared on deck. A sailor stood silhouetted before an open cabin door. Linn watched him look up at the sky.

"Ah yes, that's right!" she murmured. "The rain is wet, Master Sailor." The man retreated back into the cabin. She gathered her drenched shift and made a crouched dash down the dock, across the gangplank, and onto the ship.

Now where do I go? Farr had been a fisherman, and Linn had gone out with him once or twice. She'd only been four seasons old, but she thought there'd been a small storage area below deck on his tiny boat—the hold. She vaguely remembered teasing Farr by hiding from him there. But where was the entrance to this ship's hold? A clatter of dishes and the warm sounds of voices floated from a softly lit doorway. Linn guessed that that must be the way—the sailors would sleep and eat in the hold, especially in this weather. But she'd have to wait until everyone slept before venturing in to see if there was a lower hold below.

With her heavy, wet shift still chafing her wounds, she crept across the ship's deck, searching for a temporary place to hide. A cone-shaped pile of thick rope made a towering shadow for her to duck behind. It stank of tar and mildew. She sank gingerly to the deck, praying the rope wouldn't be needed by anyone else in the immediate future. And that Domm wouldn't take it into his head to search for her, here or anywhere else.

The ship was large by Laefe standards, long and fairly narrow and deep. A light at the ship's prow winked at Linn through the murk. She could see the curving neck of the figurehead, a black dragon with sweeping, erect wings. The enticing smell of cooked meat curled out of the galley in the stern. Her stomach twisted at the homely scent.

The sailor on watch came back out and made his rounds, brushing against her mound of rope. She held her breath and tried to sink into the decking below her. But he didn't glance down—just hustled back to the cabin's warmth after scanning the dock for intruders.

Finally, stillness settled over the ship. The storm had quieted, and now only occasional flashes of lightning lit Linn's hiding place. But just as she scuttled from her pile of rope to make a dash for the hold, voices from the muddy path above the harbor cut through the hush. Small yellow lights flickered toward the ship.

Move, move, move! The order pounded from Linn's head to her feet. She dashed through the hold door and down a wooden ladder. A shaded lantern hung on a peg at the ladder's foot, lighting the narrow landing and a tiny hall with several doors. Darkness meant safety at that moment, so she plunged into the inky recesses of the lower hold.

A stuffy mixture of scents greeted her. Apples, lumber, tar, and the yeasty, bitter odor of ale all mingled with the stifling smell of a closed-up space after a rain. But Linn had barely registered these scents before voices filtered down from the deck above. Panic shook her gut, and her recent wounds burned. The loudest voice was Domm's.

The lantern from the landing cast a weak light into the lower hold. Linn searched frantically for a hiding place. "Please, please, please, Great One," she begged under her breath. "Help me find something better than a pile of rope to hide behind!" Rough bags of flour and grain loomed over her head, while quarter- and half-barrels of cider, mead, wine, and ale stood along the sides of the hold. Linn leaned over a large barrel that smelled of apples to see how empty it was. *Tap, tap.* Cautious steps made their way down the ladder from the upper hold. She crouched behind the barrel and froze.

A pudgy boy about Carey's age hesitated in the shadowy light. A flare from the lantern above glinted off his curly hair as he peered through the gloom.

"Where are you?" he whispered. "I've only got a minute before the Ranites come down to search. They're looking for you—and they are *angry!*"

Linn's indrawn breath whistled through her teeth.

"There!" The boy darted to the barrel and grabbed her hand, yanking her upright. Without a word, he dragged Linn over to a huge pile of bulging grain sacks.

"Lie down here," he directed, trying to force her to the floor. He threw an empty sack over her as she obeyed. "Now cover your mouth and nose with your shift, and hold your breath." Picking up a sharp-looking shovel, he broke open several sacks. The grain poured out. She pulled the hem of her shift up to cover her nose. Mud from her fall glued the fabric to her cheeks, and the weight of the grain pressed her body to the decking below her. "There—you should be safe now." The boy's whisper sounded muffled through the grain. "You're completely covered. Just don't move!"

Daring only shallow breaths of dusty air, Linn strained to hear the Ranites searching the upper hold. Skeptical voices protested; demanding voices insisted. Then heavy steps clumped down the ladder into the lower hold. Icy sweat broke out on Linn's face, neck, hands, and legs, and bits of grain pricked her skin.

Pressing her face harder against the deck, she caught her breath and strained to hear what came next.

She recognized Domm's voice right away. "Yes, I realize the *Dark Dragon* is your ship, Captain Tarkin. But you're docked in our harbor, trading with our people, and we *will* search the rest of your hold!"

A higher, harder-edged voice cut across Domm's complaint. "Is that so, sirrah? I could always arrange to go elsewhere next season. If it were not so late, I'd set sail right now! But as it *is* late and you're already on board . . ." The stomp of heavy boots obscured the rest of Captain Tarkin's words.

Scraaaape. Scraaaape. A hard edge of cold metal grazed her arm. The shovel.

"What's going on here?" Tarkin demanded. "Another sack break open?"

"Yessir." The pudgy boy's voice was respectful. "The rats must've gnawed clear through a couple of 'em, and the weight split 'em open. I noticed it earlier when I came down for your wine."

"All right," the captain continued. "Get on with it, then. These gents are looking for a girl. Seen one sneak aboard tonight?"

The boy snorted. "Not too likely. Have to be crazy—out in weather like this?" Another snort, then the scraping resumed.

"Well, she might be here all the same." This was Domm, sounding sulky and barely civil. "That girl's crafty. I want to make sure she hasn't slunk aboard." His companions murmured their agreement.

The decking under Linn's cheek shook as the men searched. They poked and prodded, pushing sacks and barrels about. It didn't take long. The sound of boots stomping up the hold ladders tempted Linn to push through the grain. But a whispered "Don't move yet!" kept her still.

"Gee! Come to my cabin when you're through with that grain!" Captain Tarkin spoke from the top of the ladder. Booted feet ascended the upper ladder. *Tap tap tap. Click.*

"All right, you can come out," the boy said in a low voice. "The captain's gone now—back to his wine. You'll be safe for a bit."

An avalanche of grain rushed to the floor as Linn straightened up. A lantern placed on a low stool revealed her helper. The boy's round face was freckled and ruddy, the kind of face that was probably cheerful most of the time. But right now it looked serious.

"Thanks for helping me." Without thinking, Linn offered her wrapped hand, then winced as the boy gave it an unexpectedly strong shake. She hesitated. "I'm sorry—I have to ask—why did you do it?"

The boy turned away and shrugged. "Don't know why, really. I guess you just seemed to be in trouble." He gave her a sideways look. "I've always taken to strays."

Linn eyed his wild auburn hair and teasing expression. He seemed friendly enough. But could she trust him? *Do I have a choice?*

"My name's Linnet." She pulled a few kernels of grain from her hair. "But you can call me Linn."

"And I'm Garramond," he replied, picking up the shovel. "Everyone calls me Gee, though. I'm Captain Tarkin's son."

Four

Linn stepped back, tripping over the mound of grain. With a thud, she fell against the pile of full grain sacks behind her.

"What did you say?" she squeaked.

Gee put the business end of the shovel down into the grain and leaned against its handle, frowning. "I told you. I'm the captain's son. The cabin boy—for now, anyway."

"And *you* helped me stow away."

Gee shot her an impatient look. "Yes. I did."

"Why?" she demanded, standing upright and staring straight into Gee's eyes. They were the same auburn color as his hair. "You must tell me."

Gee held her gaze for a long minute. Then, apparently satisfied with what he saw, he nodded. "All right."

He sat down on a nearby quarter-barrel. "It was the Ranites. That's why I helped you." His face twisted in pain. "I *hate* Ranites. I saw you slipping into the hold just as the Ranites came down the hill. I could see your face in the light from the door. I could see you were afraid. And that you hated them too."

"So you're not a Ranite?"

"No." He shook his head. His mouth twisted into a sour expression. "No, that will happen when I'm fourteen seasons. At least that's what Fa tells me."

"So your father's Ranite? But then why do you hate them?"

Gee curled his hands into white-knuckled fists and slammed them down onto his knees. "I hate them because they took my father! They stole him away and changed him somehow! He's never been the same since they got hold of him!" He looked up at Linn, his eyes blazing with an odd mixture of anger, frustration, resentment, and defiance. He wiped a sleeve under his nose.

"What do you mean? How did he change?"

Gee loosed a tremulous sigh. "Fa's never been what you'd call gentle. I mean, he's a sailor, isn't he? But he was *fair*. He cared about me and my mother and my sister, Mia. But after he was persuaded to become a Ranite, he left them back in Baln—and we haven't been home for two seasons! *Two seasons!* He doesn't even talk about them anymore." Gee's face sagged. "He doesn't miss them. And now he acts as though I'm part of the rigging. I'm not a son to him—I'm just the cabin boy! All he cares about is serving Rane and wandering around trying to find some stupid city."

"*Trying* to find a city?" Linn was intrigued. "Doesn't he know where it is? It must be on his charts and maps."

"You'd think so." Gee shrugged. "But I guess not. We've been looking for it for months now. I don't know. It has to do with trees . . . the Tree City, City Tree. Something like that."

Linn caught her breath. "Your father is looking for the City of Trees?"

Gee nodded. "That's it. The City of Trees. I over-heard him talking about some people . . . leece, leez . . . lysefolk, I think he called them."

"Your father is searching for lysefolk?"

Gee nodded again, his face puzzled. "You know about them?"

Linn put her wounded hand over the Lysetome hidden in her shift. "A bit," she replied cautiously.

"What exactly *is* a lyse?"

"You don't know? He's never explained who they are?"

Gee shook his head.

Linn searched his face. He seemed sincere, but . . . Since Farr died, she'd never spoken with anyone about the Great One until she exploded at Domm. Not even Mam. That had been her one secret rebellion against her stepfather. Could she trust Gee? His eyes gazed at her, wide and unblinking. *What choice do I have? I have to trust him, whether his father is a Ranite or not.*

"My father was a Truen, a follower of the Great One. Farr believed the Great One created Maether," she told him. "He shaped it to form a cup, then filled the cup with every good thing: the sea, the land, plants, animals, fish, trees, people. Then he set twelve skjolder—strong places—to guard the world. He wanted to give gifts to the world, so he created lysefolk. Each one carried a gift, one of his favors—"

"What kind of gifts?" Gee interrupted.

"Well, knowledge of the stars and herbs and healing. The ability to speak with animals and direct the birds. The skill to read the skies and know the weather. How to farm the land, how to map it and ferment its fruit." A thrill ran through her as she spoke aloud what she had learned from Farr's Lysetome. "There's a list. Sixty gifts. Sixty lysefolk gather together in the hidden City of Trees and use their gifts so the land will prosper. Without them, their gifts, and the skjolder, all of Maether would wither and die. The Great One made them to hold the world in balance."

Gee scratched his head, leaving bits of loose grain riding atop one curly lock of hair. "But how do you know this? Where is this list?"

Linn fingered her overshift. Half reluctantly, she

pulled it out. "This is my father's book, the Lysetome. It tells the story of the Great One and his lysefolk." She opened the book and thumbed through it until she reached the listing of the gifts. "See, here it says, 'And he gave for a blessing sixty lysefolk to take what is in his mind and make it come to pass in Maether.' And then it lists the gifts."

Gee read a few lines. "You follow the Great One?" His voice was skeptical. "Fa always told me that he was nothing but a legend—he's always laughed about him with the other Ranites. Hmm." He thought for a minute. "Maybe Fa doesn't really believe that. Even though he makes fun of the Great One, he's also kind of touchy about him. Like he thinks the Great One is Rane's enemy."

Linn frowned. "He is. But what makes *you* think that?"

"A few days ago, I overheard him talking to a few of the Ranite sailors. It didn't make sense to me then. But it does now. My father's looking for the City of Trees so he can find the lysefolk. He thinks they're a threat to Rane's plans. Rane intends to rule Maether, to make everyone Ranite. Fa's been sent by Rane to destroy the lysefolk."

Linn felt the blood drain from her face. "Destroy them? But why? Why would anyone want to do that? Doesn't he realize that Rane won't have anything left to rule if he kills the lysefolk? By killing them, your father will destroy Maether, too!"

Gee's face crumpled, and he shook his head. "I don't know," he said, his voice thin and unhappy. "Fa doesn't tell me anything anymore. All I know is that he hates the lysefolk, and the Ranites are to rule Maether."

"Somehow we've got to warn the lysefolk before your father finds them!"

Gee's mouth hardened. "I can't do that."

"Why not, if you hate the Ranites too?"

"Because I love my father!" Gee brushed angry tears from his eyes. "If Rane hadn't taken him over, my father would never kill the lysefolk. He's not a murderer!" Gee bit his lower lip and it stopped trembling. When he spoke again, his voice was low and intense. "I can't desert him now. I've got to find a way to turn him from Rane. I want my real Fa back—I want to bring him back to my mother and sister. Besides"—he gave Linn a piercing look—"how do you even know the lysefolk really exist? I've never heard anyone but my father talk about them. Maybe they're just some old tale."

"They're not just an old tale! They're real!" Linn choked out, stung. "But you can't possibly save your father! Haven't you ever heard him say 'Rane does not release his own'? It's the truth! Rane will never let him go, never!"

Gee's face turned white. "How can you say that? He's

34

my father and I've got to get him back—I've just got to!" He spun around on his heel and stumbled up the hold ladder.

Linn clamped her hands over her mouth. Her skin beaded with cold sweat. "Oh, no!" It was an agonized whisper. She sank to the floor, clutching the Lysetome to her chest. "What have I done?" She sat there, trembling. What if Gee alerted the captain? What if he called Domm back to the ship? She'd spent so many years squelching her thoughts and emotions— why couldn't she have held her tongue just one more time?

The ladder to the upper hold creaked. Gee stood on the top rung. Slowly he climbed down and came to sit before her. His face was still white, but calmer. She put her wounded hand on his arm.

"I'm sorry. I didn't think. It's just that I'm scared and alone, and I don't know how to warn the lysefolk. How will I find them? I don't even know where to start. But if you and I look together, maybe we can find them— maybe save your father that way?" She gave Gee a half smile. "Can't we do it together? Please?"

"No." He shook his head and set his mouth in a stubborn line. "I've got to find a way to turn him back." His face softened a little. "But that doesn't mean I won't help you. I'll keep on spying. Maybe I'll overhear something important—maybe where my father thinks the City of Trees is. But I *won't* leave him."

Linn nodded, remembering her own dream of Farr's arms reaching for her. Wouldn't she stick as close as possible to her own father if he were still alive, no matter what?

"I understand. We can't do anything about it right now, anyway." She shivered. "But I *have* to get away from Laefe and Domm. He wants to force me to become Ranite and to wed one too!"

"Can't you talk to your mother? Wouldn't she help you—or is she Ranite, like your stepfather?"

Linn fidgeted. "No, she's not Ranite. She and Domm made an agreement before they wed. He got her dowry and she didn't have to convert." She snorted. "Fat lot of good it's done her."

"What do you mean?" Gee lowered his voice. "Is she a Truen, too?"

"She used to worship the Great One." Linn's eyes filled with tears, and she angrily brushed them away. "When I was little, when my farr was still alive, Mam was kind and gentle. She never talked about things much—she just seemed content to go along as we were. But after Farr died, she changed. All the love and kindness drained right out of her, until she was like one of these." She kicked an empty grain sack. "She didn't have anything left over for me! And when Domm asked to wed her, she didn't seem to care one way or another. Maybe she felt it was shameful not to wed again when she was so young. I don't know. Mam accepted him, and then she left me to Domm and his switch. And that suited him just fine!"

Gee looked into Linn's eyes. Suddenly he seemed much older. "I used to think being a Ranite was wonderful. But not anymore. Rane is *evil*. What does he ever do for anyone? The Ranites only want power—power over everyone and everything." A hopeless look flitted across his face. "They're sick inside," he spat.

Sick. Yes, that was the best word to describe Domm. A picture of his hard face after her switching crowded into Linn's mind, and she shivered. He enjoyed having power over her. He enjoyed making her do what went against her grain. Domm was like Rane, twisting anything in his grasp until it became ugly and distorted.

"You're right," she said. "Ranites are sick—they're *worse* than sick. They love giving themselves over to evil."

"But what can we do about it?" Gee's voice was desperate.

Linn wasn't used to doing much of anything except what she was told. Until today. She glanced over at Gee, who gazed back at her hopefully. Whatever it was, something was different. Inside her. *I can do something—I will do something! But what?* She thought about the plant-path and the tugging sensation that had drawn her along it. These things must mean something—something good. She could pledge herself to them—to whatever worked against Rane. Somehow, some way, she would find the hidden City of Trees, seek out the lyse-folk. Maybe this plant-path could help her. Someone had to warn the lysefolk of the Ranites' intention.

The wound on Linn's hand throbbed. And those thin-yet-strong threads were back, pulling gently but insistently on her insides.

"Linn? What's the matter? Is something wrong? You look odd."

Linn opened her mouth, then paused. A wonderful sense of deep approval washed through her. She felt strong, daring, full of purpose. Hope bubbled up until her chest felt tight with it. She smiled at Gee. "Just help me stow away. Then we'll see if the Great One won't help us change what the Ranites intend—for Maether *and* your father."

Gee's forehead creased. Then, with a look of dawning hope, he slowly nodded.

Five

Linn rolled back and forth in the dark, cradling her stomach as it clenched at the violent movement of the ship. A vile smell rose from the bucket by her feet.

"Only five days on board—who'd have thought I'd get so seasick?" she moaned. "Ohhh." She made it to the bucket just in time. She mopped her face with a smelly cloth and leaned back. When would this nightmare end?

She dragged herself over to a leather waterskin and took a small drink, just enough to wash some of the taste from her mouth. The pile of biscuits and smallcakes Gee had smuggled down lay shoved aside. Their smell made Linn's stomach lurch again. She rolled over and lay prone against the side of the little hideyhole Gee had made for her from some old sacks and boards.

Quiet footsteps and a bobbing light invaded her misery. Gee's head appeared in the hidey-hole's opening, his hair glinting in the glow of the lantern he raised.

"No better? Sorry!" He looked disgustingly cheerful and well. "I warned you how the Midwaters are—they make even the heartiest sailor sick!" He lowered his voice, even though no one could overhear. "Fa heard a rumor on Wheat Isle, a few days before we docked in Laefe. He thinks the City might be hidden somewhere in Northain, maybe along the coast."

Linn groaned.

"In a day or so we'll dock in Sand. It's the largest Northain city—well, actually it's the *only* town in Northain that can really be called a city." He grinned, and Linn smiled back weakly.

"Sand's a wonderful place," Gee continued, dumping the contents of her swill bucket into a larger one he'd brought along. "The market is full of merchants, selling everything from musical instruments to cloth woven with gold. There are puppet shows and poetry contests and open-air taverns with the most delicious food! I'll sneak you ashore somehow."

Linn tried to smile again through tightly clenched teeth. *I will not retch, I will not retch,* she told herself grimly.

He peered at her, an anxious look on his face. Apparently reassured, he continued. "Fa's planning to meet with a group of Ranites there." Gee rolled his eyes. "He's hoping they'll know more about where he can find the City of Trees. If I'm lucky, I can spy on his meeting. Maybe I'll learn something valuable."

He crouched next to Linn. She made a supreme effort of will and sat up. Gee drew something out of his tunic. "Thanks again for lending me your Lysetome. I took it up to the crow's nest and read some of it yesterday. I suppose you want it back now?"

Linn nodded and reached out to take the book. But Gee held on to it, stroking the leather cover. "You can't really read down here, you know. It's too dark." His eyes pleaded with her. "Do you think maybe I could keep it for a bit longer? I just got to the part where the Great One meets Maer by the lake."

"Oh, I don't know," Linn said, doubt in her voice. "It was my father's, and . . . and . . ." She trailed off.

Gee's shoulders drooped, and he thrust the Lysetome at Linn. She took it, feeling selfish and mean. He'd already done so much for her.

She hesitated, then steeled herself. "Here, take it. But please be careful. It's the only thing I have left from my farr." Gee gave her a solemn nod and slipped the book back inside his tunic.

Creak.

"Shhh." Gee put a finger to his lips and kept his voice low. "That's the top rung. Someone's coming."

"Gee? Are you down there, boy?"

"It's Fa!" Gee scrambled quickly to his feet, motioning for Linn to keep quiet. He clambered across piles of apples and tubers, making for the hold's ladder. Tarkin's boots shook the wooden rungs. Linn crept forward and peeked around a barrel to see Gee bending over to pick up a broom. *Fwack!* Something flopped to the floor in front of him. She drew in a sharp breath. No—it couldn't be!

But it was. The Lysetome lay exposed in a little puddle of light cast by the lantern. Gee snatched the book from the floor and furtively tried to stuff it back in his tunic. Too late.

"What are you doing, boy?" Tarkin swung down the ladder and grabbed Gee's wrist.

Linn shoved the smelly rag in her mouth to keep from crying out. *Don't let him take my Lysetome!*

Tarkin yanked the book from Gee's hands, pushing the boy away when he tried to grab it back. The captain's bushy black eyebrows twisted into a frowning tangle.

"A Lysetome? You have a Lysetome, boy?" His hand flashed out, and a ringing smack filled the air as it met Gee's ear. "And just what in Rane's name do you think you're doing with it?" Tarkin grabbed Gee by the collar of his tunic and shook him. "Answer me right now! Where did you get this?"

Gee shrank from his father but shook his head. Tarkin's hand shot up for another slap. "No, Fa!" Gee cried, covering his head and ducking, deflecting the blow.

"All right! You won't tell me the easy way, boy, so we'll have to get it out of you the hard way." He flung Gee over a nearby half-barrel and raised the Lysetome above his head, ready to bring it crashing down on the boy's backside.

For a split second, Linn froze. She was back in the stedyard, cowering in the dirt. Domm raised his arm and the switch came whistling toward her.... "Nooo!" Linn burst from her hiding place and flung herself against Tarkin. The book hit her shoulder and fell to the floor as the captain staggered back.

She seized the Lysetome and thrust it down her shift. "Come on!" She grabbed Gee's hand and dragged him up the ladder to the deck.

"Where are you two goin'?" A huge, burly sailor with a Ranite tattoo blocked their way, and the captain appeared in the doorway behind them, wheezing from his pursuit.

"Good job, Urse." Tarkin made a motion, and Urse dropped a heavy hand on each fugitive's shoulder. The captain gave the pair a hard stare, then began to pace back and forth, his forefinger stroking his upper lip. His Ranite mark—the twin of Domm's red circle tattoo—smoldered faintly in the dusk, reflecting light from the lantern. Finally, he stopped and glared at Linn.

"You stowed away, eh? You must be Domm's child, then."

"I am *not* Domm's child!" Linn returned hotly. "He wed my mother, but that doesn't make him my father!"

Tarkin waved a hand dismissively. "All right, then. He's your *step*father. But I want to know how the kin of a Ranite possesses a Lysetome." He stared pointedly at the front of Linn's shift. "Because I know my son never had one before you came aboard."

Linn compressed her lips. Better to say nothing than too much. She snatched a look at Gee out of the corner of her eye. His face sagged with misery. *He loves his father—even if Tarkin beats him. How can he?* She thought about how she would feel if her own farr had beaten her, and shuddered. It was bad enough when Domm did it. *There must be something in there to love. What is it?*

"Well? Speak up, girl—answer me!"

"Why should I?"

Tarkin's eyes narrowed. "Because if you don't, your new friend here will pay." Slowly he unbuckled his tunic belt.

"Don't hurt him!" She wrapped her arms around her chest, clasping the Lysetome for strength. "You're a coward to hit a boy. *My* father was a Truen, not a cur of a Ranite." Linn spat on the deck.

Tarkin sneered. "Your father followed the Great One? Ha! And I suppose he thought himself a lyse?" Linn's eyes dropped to the deck, and she bit her lip to keep from blurting out what she longed to tell him.

He began his pacing once more. "The lysefolk are

doomed, you know. What few there are left, anyway. The Great One has deserted Maether. Rane alone is supreme. That book contains only superstition and lies fit to deceive the very young and very foolish, like you."

He paused, fixing Linn with his gaze. "You will be returned to your family. But not immediately. I have a mission to complete that is more important than returning a runaway to her father, even if he is a Ranite. But I'll keep you safe in the brig until then. When you return, your stepfather can resume his plans for you. And from what he's told me, they will *not* include the Great One."

Tarkin reached out and ran a horny finger down her cheek. Linn jerked away. A disagreeable smile flitted across the captain's face. "Oh, no. A fine Ranite husband awaits you back on Laefe. So you *will* return. My honor as a follower of Rane demands that."

Linn's stomach, already shaky from days of vomiting, twisted. Suddenly everything receded into the distance. Despising herself, she began slipping slowly to the deck. The last thing she saw before unconsciousness took her was the despairing look on Gee's round, freckled face.

Six

"**S**he's been sick, Fa." Gee's voice filtered through to Linn from far, far away. "She's weak from throwing up."

The bitter bite of sea air helped rouse Linn from her faint. That and the cold night wind that blew across the *Dark Dragon's* deck. Lanterns cast a wavering light on Gee's face floating anxiously above her. He helped her struggle into a sitting position. The movement made Linn's head spin.

Tarkin motioned for a sailor to bring Linn the steaming cup he held in his hand, his foot tapping the deck impatiently. It turned out to be hot tea, loaded with honey. She drank greedily, watching Tarkin over the cup's rim. Then she set the cup on the deck, wiping her mouth with the back of her right hand.

Without warning, Tarkin swooped down and snatched Linn's hand with his raspy fingers, turning it so her palm was exposed to the lantern's light. His stale breath brushed her cheek, and his hands began to shake, "Impossible!" He dropped her hand as though it burned him, backing away into the shadows. The red tattoo on his forehead flickered at Linn in the darkness.

She staggered to her feet. "What's the matter? What's wrong?" She stumbled over to the lantern and examined her right hand in its wavering light. The wound on her palm looked as fresh as the day it had been made, a straight, angry red line almost like an arrow. It stretched from her wrist to her middle finger, capped by a small triangle where the switch had cut away a hunk of skin.

"I don't understand," she mumbled, looking up at Tarkin. "What did you see?"

Tarkin's hand came up, warding her off as if she were a demon. "You're the one," he rasped, his voice shaking. "You are the *one!*"

Linn stared at Gee, who shrugged. She turned to the sailors standing in a semicircle around them. A wave of their scent—sweat and dirt and tar—rolled over her. The ones closest to her bore the red Ranite tattoo on their foreheads, but she took a step toward them anyway and stretched out her hand.

"What is he talking about?" she begged. "Do you understand what he means?"

Once more the lantern lit up Linn's outstretched palm. The Ranite sailors backed away, arms raised protectively and eyes fixed in fascinated horror on her hand. A few gasped. Finally Urse pushed through the crowd and took Linn's hand into his huge, leathery paw. She tried to yank it back, but he held fast.

He grunted, then looked over at Tarkin, his face unexpectedly shrewd. "She's the one, right enough," he concluded, dropping her hand. "What're you going to do about it, Cap'n?"

Urse's pronouncement stiffened Tarkin's spine. His face still looked pale in the lantern's light, but he approached Linn and took her hand once more. He gazed long and hard at the wound before letting her hand fall.

"You are the one, girl," he repeated. A muscle twitched in his left eyelid. "You are the one Rane's farsight spoke of. You have the mark of the Arrow, the Hidden Arrow, on your palm." Linn stared at him, her face blank. "Rane spoke of the Hidden Arrow in a farsight, a prophecy. The Arrow is a danger to all things Ranite—it's a curse from the Great One! Don't you know a lysemark when you see it?"

Linn staggered back as though the man had hit her in the face. "A lysemark? It can't be a lysemark." Her voice was faint and husky. "It's just a scar from my stepfather's last beating." She stared at the wound, then slowly murmured her thoughts aloud, forgetting the men around her. "And what does Rane know, anyway? He's just a lying demon, not a god."

Urse charged forward, palm poised to smack her.

Tarkin held up a hand. "Wait. That's not an accidental scar, girl, despite what you think of Rane. It's a lyse-mark, no matter how it got there. The question is, what do I do with you?" For a few moments he paced the deck again, his forefinger caressing one heavy black eyebrow. Finally he came to a dead halt, fear and hesitation wiped from his face.

"The farsight cannot be fulfilled without the Hidden Arrow. Am I right, men?" The Ranites murmured agreement. "We could kill her." Gee took a step forward, his face flushing dark red. Tarkin waved him back. "We *could* kill her. But instead, why not create a *Ranite* Arrow?"

The Ranite crewmembers paused to consider this idea. Urse stroked his chin, nodding, his mouth gradually forming a sneer. "Time for the circle, eh, Cap'n?"

"Yes, Urse. I think it is."

The crew spread out to form a large ring, with the Ranite sailors claiming the inner positions. Linn, held tight in Urse's grip, shivered inside the circle. A crewmember brought a brazier forward and loaded it with coals, lighting them with a white-hot coal another fetched from the galley.

When the sharp smell of dry heat rose from the brazier, Tarkin produced an iron ring and carefully bound it around an assortment of strange-looking herbs. Then he dipped them in a metal cup offered by a Ranite sailor and laid the dripping herbs on the brazier's coals.

A sizzling cloud of steam shot up. Another sailor stepped forward, proffering Tarkin an ornately decorated metal jar and a cock's tail feather. Tarkin dipped the feather into the jar and began to draw symbols on the deck around the brazier and Linn. The light glinted off the symbols, a deep red color. Was there blood in that jar?

When he'd finished, the Ranite sailors started to chant, an eerie, guttural sound in a language Linn didn't recognize. One sailor extinguished the lantern. Their tattoos gleamed in the darkness.

At first, it seemed that the fire had gone out. But soon it began to heat up again. Linn's nose twitched, and her nostrils flared with distaste. The smoke from the brazier smelled sweet and cloying, and for a second she wondered if someone had thrown a piece of rotting animal flesh on the fire. Then, so gradually that she wasn't at all sure she'd really seen anything, something dark and smoky writhed out of the brazier and across the deck.

The wind that whipped Linn's hair across her face had no effect on the smoky thing. It crept down from the brazier to the deck, quick and liquid and somehow almost alive with malevolence. The smoke seemed more real than the deck or the ship or even the sailors standing in a circle around it. Linn could see each individual wisp reach out toward her, could feel its desire pulsing against her skin as it slithered to her. It wound around, wider and wider, until it formed a spiral whose center was a hungry, empty hole into nothingness.

Now the circle of smoke brushed Linn's legs, leaving them sticky and raw with cold. The iciness crept up her thighs and torso, and she struggled against it until it clutched at her throat. Horror turned her heart to water. *Rane is real! He's here—he's come for me!* She tried to twist away, to turn and hide her face in Urse's fat stomach, to touch something human and ordinary. But the smoke's freezing grip held her fast.

The smoke began to lift from the deck, twisting into a human shape. Only this shape was taller than any man, than *two* men, towering above Linn, barely contained by the sailors' circle. A spiral of smoke detached itself from the main column, stretching down toward the brazier. As it approached the coals, the smoke resolved itself into a huge, beautifully proportioned silver arm.

The rest of the column began to pulse and shift. Greasy darkness transformed into a light-filled pillar of mist, which in turn formed a huge silvery figure. A beautiful figure, viewed through what seemed to Linn a brilliantly lit layer of ice.

She gasped. Was there movement under that icy surface? Her breath came quicker as the mist thinned and revealed a bit more of the beautiful thing within. The figure was glorious! If only she could reach through the mist and touch it . . .

The arm was so distinct that Linn could count the

individual silver hairs on its fingers, fingers each longer than Linn's forearm. They reached into the brazier and, unaffected by its heat, delicately sifted through the coals to pick up the iron ring that had bound the herbs. The ring glowed red-hot against the being's fingertips.

Then the figure turned toward Linn, unhurried and deliberate. It held the fire-ruddy ring between its forefinger and thumb, just at the height of her forehead.

The shape bent tenderly toward her. Benevolence and kindness rolled off it, embracing Linn's frozen body. Now the figure's icy covering began to melt, running onto the deck like rainwater in the spring. Linn's heart fluttered against her rib cage. If only she could touch it, be touched by this graceful, perfect being! She forgot about Gee, about Tarkin, about the lysefolk, and even about her own farr. She only wanted the radiant being swaying toward her.

Then its face burst free from the melting ice. It was the face of a silver god, noble and serious and serenely intelligent. It smiled deeply into Linn's eyes, full of promise and concern, offering answers to all her problems. Her chest swelled with hope and life until she thought her heart would burst.

Against the wide part of her back, Urse gave a hard little laugh. Then Rane—for the silver god *must* be he— spoke.

"Open thy mouth, daughter, and receive thy master."

Rane's silvery lips parted. Linn did not yet obey, instead looking expectantly into the wide mouth. A smell, nauseating and decayed, drifted down to her. The odor of death. In a flash, Rane's mouth transformed into a blackened maw, an open grave, and from it spiraled a whorl of dark mist, ready to take possession of Linn, body and soul.

Seven

"Noooo! No, you can't!"

Linn erupted from her frozen state and scrabbled frantically at Urse's bulk. "Time to meet your master, girl," he murmured in her ear, pushing her forward. Despite the cold wind, sweat poured down her face, and her forehead burned in anticipation of that red-hot circle of iron.

The dark mist of Rane wound its way toward her head, lazily spiraling around it as though embracing her. Linn flinched back, mouth shut tight. Urse took her head in his hands, clamping it between them to steady it for the touch of the slowly encroaching iron circle.

Clunk! Fwoosh!

Rane vanished in a blink as a shower of fire blazed across the deck. Linn turned and saw Gee struggling against Tarkin's angry grasp, his feet kicking at the overturned brazier. Burning coals scattered everywhere, and the tar-soaked decking was already on fire.

"Gee! You saved—" Urse yanked Linn off her feet and dragged her to the ship's rail. He dropped her arm to grab a bucket of salt water that stood ready for the next swabbing. Then he careened across the deck, chasing sparks and flames.

"Watch out, Linn!" Gee cried, still wriggling in his father's clasp. "Watch out!"

Tarkin's head jerked up, his eyes locked on Linn's. He ground his teeth. "Grab her! Don't let her get away!" Urse dropped his bucket and charged toward her, brushing aside sailors as if they were broomsticks.

Linn's head whipped back and forth, searching for a way out. She clambered onto the deck rail, heart hammering and body swaying in the buffeting wind. Below her, huge waves slapped against the ship, traveling mountains whose valleys dipped into nothingness. She turned back to Tarkin.

"Better a dead Truen than a living Ranite!" she screamed into the wind. Then she closed her eyes and jumped.

"Aagh!" Heart-freezing water closed over her head. She struggled to return to the rough surface, the wound on her palm erupting in pain as the salt water poured into it. Her gasping breaths sounded loud, despite the crashing waves. The ship! She jerked her head around.

The *Dark Dragon* already bobbed far away. Linn floated alone in the Midwaters.

"What have I done?" she whimpered into the darkness. Automatically, her arms and legs began to paddle after the *Dark Dragon*. A wave slapped over her head and pulled her under. She struggled to the surface again, thrashing against the water in her terror. Water spewed back up her throat, and salt burned her eyes and mouth. But the pain cleared a tiny space in her mind and helped her force back her panic. She dragged deep drafts of night air into her lungs. It was like breathing in broken glass, but it sharpened her thoughts.

The *Dark Dragon* wouldn't come back for her. By the time they'd put out the deck fire, the ship would be too far away to turn about. They probably thought she was already dead.

The Midwaters' cold seized her, biting deep into her bones. Her chattering teeth mimicked her thoughts. *What to do, what to do?* "O-oh, F-Farr. I w-wish y-you were h-here n-now!" *But he's not.* The finality of that thought clanged in her head. *So what will you do?*

There was only one thing to do. To stay alive, she'd have to swim for Northain.

Shaking uncontrollably, she floated on her back to get her bearings by the stars. Directly overhead winked the Polstar, around which the whole array of the night sky unfolded. Linn located the Hunter, poised eternally to shoot his twinkling silver arrow to the north. Then, with only the cold sea to buoy her, she set off.

The waves of the Midwaters rose menacingly above her one second, only to flip her off a crest the next. Within minutes Linn's limbs dragged. Her shift was heavy with salt water. Every stroke demanded a huge effort of will, a struggle against the cry of her body to just give up and sink into the depths.

After a while, the rhythm of her arms pushing through the water became hypnotic. Torpid warmth caressed her body, and the waves pounded her over and over with a single message: *sleep, sleep, sleep.* Linn began to slip beneath the surface. She was almost grateful when a wave pulled her under.

She sank slowly into the depths, half-unconscious, until something tapped her head. Jerking fully awake, she stared. A face gazed at her through the murky sea. A hairy face with eyes that glowed. In a wink it disappeared, and something hard, yet curiously warm, too, took hold of each wrist. A second later, her pelvis lifted. Then the water was rushing past her, and her face erupted into the cold night.

Linn gulped air frantically, finding that she did, after all, want to live. She peered through dripping strands of hair. To her right, something large, sleek, and sinewy held her wrist in its mouth. Sharp teeth glinted in the moon's light. A similar, much lighter-colored figure had hold of her left wrist. Long tails as thick as Linn's upper forearm wound back and forth, propelling her easily through the waves.

Behind her, two more sleek shapes nosed into place, pressing close to her sides. Gradually, a little of the creatures' body warmth transferred to Linn, and she could feel her limbs again.

On and on . . . The night swim was an endless dream. Moonlight bled all color from the creatures. The stars overhead flickered down on them as they thrust up and down each towering wave. They never seemed to tire, but Linn's muscles grew numb and heavy again until she sank into a stupor.

Finally, her chest scraped across something hard. "Wh-wha—?" She pushed herself up with her wounded hand and winced. She lay atop a huge, flat rock, half in, half out of the freezing water. Was that a beach? Hope brought her heart into her throat, and bit by bit she dragged her body across the rock and onto a sandy shore. Her face hit the ground, grating against a carpet of sand, pebbles, and broken shells. Then the blessed relief of a long, exhausted sleep overcame her.

"No, stop! It's not time to get up, Carey!" She brushed a hand across her face. Drops of water from her sleeve peppered her cheek. Her eyelids felt as heavy as granite, but she forced them up. Daylight blinded her, and she blinked. "Oh—not home. The *Dark Dragon*, that's right. I escaped." She tried to push herself up-right, but couldn't move her body or legs. Something heavy and warm weighed them down.

A face popped up before her. An animal's whiskery, blunt face, with sleek russet fur and liquid brown eyes. *"Chirrup?"* It moved closer and tickled her with its tough whiskers. Linn brought her hand up to scratch the animal's rounded jaw.

Then a tiny earthquake shook Linn's body. A weight rolled off her, allowing her to sit up. Eight similar animals sat all around her. They had been lying on top of her, keeping her warm.

For a moment they gazed stolidly at the being they had rescued. Then they began grooming their long, well-muscled bodies, their thick, strong necks bending toward powerful forelegs and blunt forepaws. The animals' sleek fur ranged in color from dark mahogany to pale auburn.

The first animal, smaller and much younger-looking than the others, ambled back to Linn with a fish. To her surprise, the sight of it brought a gush of saliva to her mouth. Wishing with all her heart she had a fire to cook it on, Linn steeled herself to take a bite. The raw flesh squeaked unpleasantly against her teeth, and the scales felt hard—as if she were chewing on fingernails. Determined, she spat them out and sank her teeth back into the fish's firm coolness. "Mmm. Salty." The animal brought her several raw birds' eggs next, pushing them along the sand with its blunt nose. She cracked them open, and albumen dripped from her fingers, a disgusting, slimy mess. Even so, the eggs slid easily down her throat.

A brisk breeze off the water brought goose bumps to Linn's wet skin. Shakily she rose to her feet and looked around. Had she come ashore in Northain? Not that knowing where she was would actually help. She wanted to find the City of Trees, but what hope did she have? Even the Ranites couldn't find it.

Linn looked at the group of self-possessed animals before her. Maybe they could help? "Where should I go?" she asked the biggest one. "I thank you kindly for your aid, but I can't stay here or I'll die."

The stately red-gold animal remained seated, staring impassively at Linn. Then, one by one, the others slipped over the sand and back into the sea. Only the largest and the smallest stayed behind. The little one trotted over to a rock and picked up something flat and brown. It dropped the object at her feet.

"My Lysetome!" Linn scooped it up and riffled through it. Completely wet, of course, and stained with salt. But the ink still looked legible—it hadn't bled too much. Gratefully, Linn secured it inside her damp shift front.

There was only one way to get warm: walk briskly. Turning her back on the bay, Linn climbed up the narrow sand beach on shaky legs to stand shivering in the tough grass just above it. She closed her eyes. "Great One! Help me, please!" Then she raised her lids, hardly daring to hope for an answer.

Nothing. Well, what did she expect? Linn sighed, clutching the Lysetome. What she wouldn't give to see even Carey's smirking face just now! Or Gee's freckled smile—

Suddenly the skin covering her ribs tensed. And then that tingling, pulling sensation she'd felt on Laefe swept across her stomach. The threads were back, demanding her attention. Their imperious jolts made her ribs ache with the need to follow them to the northeast. Linn took one cautious step forward.

As soon as her foot touched the tough grasses before her, the individual stems bent low to the ground. Then, as if a carpet were being shaken out, a rippling mass of plants bowed low before her, forming a distinct path that stretched yards ahead. Linn took three more steps. The path rolled out farther. She glanced over her shoulder. The grasses behind her resumed their normal position, tossing back and forth in the wind as the grasses on Laefe had.

"Is *this* your answer?" Linn breathed.

She felt a bump on the back of her knee. It was the younger of the two animals, pushing its blunt head against her leg. It looked up at her, its brown eyes eager.

"Chirr, chirrup!" It pushed again. The red-gold beast remained detached, leaving the decision up to her.

"Well, I don't really have much of a choice, do I?" Linn smiled at the young animal. She stepped out on the path, wondering what in Maether it would bring.

Eight

Squatting at the edge of a small grove of trees, Linn gnawed at the tough, bitter bulb of a wild leek. *"Ptoo! Pah!"* She spat out a moldy part but doggedly continued chewing. The fish and eggs supplied by the small animal had lasted long enough for her to follow the path first northeast, then due east away from the beach, carrying the animal most of the way. She had been just about frantic with hunger when she'd spied the leek and garlic patch.

Linn's eyes watered from the leek, and she rubbed a damp sleeve across her face. *I wish there were a stream nearby.* She licked her salt-dried lips and sighed. The large animal sat atop a pile of dead ferns near the grove's edge, while the smaller one pressed against Linn's back. Its body heat radiated into her.

"Aah," she murmured, her lids closing. She struggled

to stay awake. "Come here." She carried the smaller animal over to the older one. Then she snuggled down between them and slept.

The musky whiskers of the smaller animal roused her a few minutes later. "I know, I know—time to go," she grumbled. She rose and stretched her back, hands raised high above her head. The sleep—and the leeks— had done her some good. "Ready."

The path rolled out before her again. But after a step or two, Linn paused, ears straining to hear. *Snuffle, snuffle. Grunt.* She turned. A strong odor of pig and rotting feces assaulted her nose. The tall grasses behind her shook and then parted.

"It's a boar! Run!" she shrieked. Obediently, one animal veered off to the right and the other to the left. The shaggy boar ignored them and headed straight for Linn.

Go, go, go! She didn't know when she'd started to run. Nothing existed apart from red pig eyes, gleaming ivory tusks, pounding hooves, and her own gasping breath. Her hands clutched at her wet shift. Her heart banged wildly in her chest.

A tree appeared magically before her, a tree on the edge of a thick forest. She leaped for the lowest branch and wrapped her legs around it.

The boar pranced below her on ridiculously dainty hooves, slobber flecking its jowls. *Snap! Snap!* It jumped up and slashed Linn's dangling shift. She yanked the garment away and tucked it between her legs with one hand, shoving the end of her plait securely into her mouth for good measure. Then, slowly and cautiously, she righted herself and climbed to a higher branch.

Panting and wincing at the stitch that had developed in her side, Linn gazed down on the frustrated boar. It nosed about a bit, searching for a way to get at its prey. After a few moments of snuffling at the foot of the tree, it gave up and trotted reluctantly away into the forest.

As soon as the boar disappeared, Linn's animal companions cautiously broke cover and made their way to the foot of her tree. Linn abandoned her roost, landing with a thud. She leaned against the tree, shakily sliding down until she was sitting on the ground. The smaller animal curled solicitously around her neck, nuzzling her face with its whiskery cheek. The other animal sat facing the pair, its gaze solemn and limpid. Linn stretched out her still-shaking hand to tickle the area behind its flat ears.

"I don't recall ever seeing anyone run quite that fast," said a voice above her. "Nor climb a tree so quickly."

Linn clambered to her feet, her heart lurching. She stood on tiptoe to peer up through the branches of the tree. Nothing.

"Hello?" she inquired, hands pressed against the tree's rough bark.

"Oh—so sorry," the disembodied voice continued, a

hint of laughter behind the politely apologetic words. "I guess you didn't know I was here. Wait. I'm coming down." The tree branches rustled slightly.

Emerging slowly from the mass of autumn-orange leaves, as though out of nowhere, came a pair of gray eyes. They fixed on Linn, darting sideways to take in the two animals next to her.

More rustling. A man swung down to perch on a branch just above Linn. She took a step back to get a better look. The gray eyes looked out from beneath black eyebrows. His straight, black hair, gathered securely at the nape of his neck with a piece of leather, was streaked with white and silver. Even so, Linn guessed he wasn't much older than twenty seasons.

Apparently deciding that Linn didn't pose much of an immediate threat, he leaped down from the branch, landing with a soft thump. He smiled without showing his teeth, and his long, narrow face widened, making his large nose much less prominent. "Like what you see?" he asked with a lifted eyebrow.

"I haven't decided yet."

He shrugged. "Now it's my turn." He slowly circled her. *He might as well be examining a donkey he intends to buy,* Linn thought, rankled. Her shoulders twitched, and she ducked her head away from his probing eyes.

"Hmm." He reached out and pulled a bit of kelp from her hair. "What have you been doing with your-

self? All covered with nasty bits of sand and leaves—
and damp, too. But no matter. I guess you could use
some food, some drink, a wash-up, and a good sleep.
Correct?"

She hesitated, but the thought of food overcame her
reluctance and she nodded, just as a pathetic rumble
erupted from her midsection. She clapped her hands
over her complaining stomach, mortified.

He grinned. "Well, how far do you think you can
walk?"

"As far as I have to."

The young man bent down to retrieve a small leather
wallet from a knot of grasses at the base of the tree.
"Come along, then," he said, indicating the direction he
wanted to go. "My blind's not too far away."

Linn and the two animals trudged behind him into
the forest. Her wet shift snagged on every passing bush.
"Ow!" she cried as a low-growing branch flicked her
neck. She rubbed the sore place and felt something wet
on her hand. Blood.

"You all right?" He stopped to wait for her.

"Yes."

"Need any help?"

"No!" It sounded explosive in the quiet woods. "No.
I'm fine." Quieter this time. "Let's just keep going."

"Not necessary. We're already here."

Linn took a few steps forward and stood next to him.
"Where is it? It's just a tiny clearing."

He grinned. "Come on. You'll see." He gestured to a small clump of trees, bushes, and vines. "Welcome to my blind."

Linn walked over and reached out to touch the vine-covered trunks. "How clever! You've filled the spaces between a circle of trees with split logs and covered them with vines! I wouldn't have known it was here!"

"It took a while to build, but it was worth the effort. I like my privacy."

He led Linn and the two animals around to the other side of the blind. A tall bush hid the entrance. Linn ducked low and squeezed past it to enter. Small, carefully placed openings in the vine-covered thatched roof let in some light, and a small stone hearth sheltered a tiny fire.

"Don't you get wet when it rains?" Linn pointed to the openings.

He shook his head. "No. I've arranged the vines over them so that only the occasional drop or two gets in. Of course, I do have to cut the vines back or they'd grow right down my walls."

He waved her to a rough stool near the hearth. Linn sat down, cuddling the smaller animal on her lap. She stretched her hands out to the snug fire, basking in its warmth. Her companion threw on a log, then began to set out a meal. He put an earthenware pitcher of grog to warm on the hearth, then took flatbread, creamy cheese, dried fruit, and nuts out of a wooden box and set them before Linn.

She swallowed hard, and her stomach growled again. "Thank you," she squeaked, then fell on the food.

It was fare she was used to eating at home, but it tasted like a feast today. She devoured a large chunk of cheese, three small rounds of flatbread, and a cup of nuts in short order.

Her host's eyes widened. "Here, have more." He handed her another hunk of cheese and a handful of fruit. The mug of grog he poured for her disappeared in one long gulp.

"Well now—satisfied? How about a nice wash?"

Linn hesitated again, but the thought of being clean overcame her reluctance to trust the young man. She nodded.

"Here's soap, a jug of hot water, a basin, and a flannel." He dug around in a pack propped against the wall. "And here are some fresh clothes. I doubt yours are worth washing, and anyway, I'm not set up for laundry here. No tub. Come on, you two." He waved the animals to the door. "Fish outside."

Left alone, Linn stripped off her wet clothes and scrubbed herself briskly all over with soap and hot water, rubbing herself dry with the flannel. Then she washed her hair. It felt heavenly, even if it wasn't the clean of a good, hot bath.

She shrugged into the waiting clothing: two warm woolen shirts, a heavy tunic, wool leggings, and some curious shoes that started out as flat pieces of flexible leather before snugly wrapping around her feet with laces. All were the same brown-green color as the clothes her host wore. Linn plaited her hair and tied it with a bit torn from her discarded shift. She hesitated, then carefully balanced the Lysetome, spine vertical and pages fanned, behind a small pile of wood by the hearth to dry. "You'll be safe there," she whispered.

She picked up the basin of filthy water and made a face. "Ugh," she said, then stood in the blind's doorway and flung the water in a wide arc, narrowly missing the young man as he returned with the animals.

Linn dropped the basin and opened her mouth to apologize and thank him, but he laid a forefinger across his smiling lips. "Next comes sleep. Talk can wait." He pointed to a small mattress atop a neat pile of leaves and ferns. Obedient through exhaustion, Linn lay down and pulled a thick woolen blanket over her.

The fire crackled quietly, casting lightly moving shadows on the blind's walls. The young man took out a reed whistle and piped a quiet tune. It made Linn think of birds settling their feathers for a rest, still and comforting and homey.

"May I ask you just one question?" she murmured dreamily.

"Ask ahead," he said, removing the whistle from his lips.

"Your name?"

"My name is Thom. Now sleep."

And she did.

Nine

"Mmmm." Linn rolled over. A delicious aroma tickled her nose, and she sat up. A small wooden bowl with a damp cloth over it stood on the hearth. Linn lifted the cloth. "Mmmm," she repeated. Porridge with dried fruit and honey, warm and fragrant. She ate hungrily, washing everything down with scalding hot tea from the kettle suspended over the fire. Then she knelt down next to the woodpile and reached behind it.

No soggy leather binding, no brittle pages. Nothing but dried-up bits of bark and slivers of wood. Her heart in her mouth, Linn scrabbled through the pile of small logs. Nothing! She sagged against the stones surrounding the hearth.

There was only one answer. "Thom!" She sprang to her feet and slammed out of the blind. He wasn't in the clearing. She saw the smaller of the two animals lying curled up in a pile of leaves and bent to scoop him up. A clear, short whistle floated down from somewhere overhead. Thom peered at her through branches that still retained their golden-brown leaves. He held up a finger, then, with an amazingly quiet movement, slid down the tree trunk and landed silently at her feet.

"Where is my Lysetome?" Linn burst out, clutching the animal.

"*Wheek!*" the animal yelped in protest of her rough treatment.

Thom frowned. "You shouldn't treat a kjaerdyr like that!" He reached to take the animal from her.

Linn jerked away. "Where is my Lysetome? Why did you take it?" Her eyes narrowed. "Are you a Rane worshiper?"

Thom threw back his head and laughed. "Worship Rane? Hardly." He retrieved something from a stump near the blind. "Here's your precious Lysetome. I just brought it out here to dry more slowly. The fire was making the pages brittle."

Linn snatched the book from him and riffled through it. The pages did seem a bit fragile, and the leather cover had swollen and started to pull away from its thin vellum lining. But the Lysetome was basically intact. "Thank the Great One!"

"Yes, thank him that a thief like me didn't make off with it in the night!"

Warmth flooded Linn's face, and she pressed the animal's russet fur against her cheek. "I'm sorry, Thom. I panicked. It belonged to my father."

"Hmm. Your father had a Lysetome. And you invoke the Great One. I think we should have that talk now."

They went back into the blind, and Thom poured two mugs of tea. "All right, I will begin. Who are you and where do you come from?"

Linn fingered the Lysetome. He'd sheltered her, fed her, yes. But should she trust him? She stared at him, weighing her options.

He returned her gaze without blinking. "What do you have to lose?"

Everything. One thing was certain: she needed help. No food, no water, no equipment, no transportation but her own two legs. Did she really have a choice?

She took a deep breath. "My name is Linn—Linnet, really. I came from Laefe aboard a ship called the *Dark Dragon*. My real father is dead, and my stepfather planned to betroth me to a Ranite." She shot a covert look at him. Was he sympathetic to Rane? No change. "He is a Ranite. He beat me, so I stowed away."

Thom wrapped his arms around his knees, his gray eyes bright with curiosity. And something more . . . something Linn couldn't read.

"But how did you end up *here*?"

"Where *is* here?"

"You're in Northain now, just a week's journey east of Sand."

"Oh." Linn nodded, stroking the animal in her lap. Hesitantly, she told Thom about Tarkin's assertion that she was the Hidden Arrow of Rane's farsight. "He tried to force me to become Ranite. They called up Rane." Linn closed her eyes and clutched the animal tightly to her chest. She swallowed. "He—it—came. It spoke to me and told me it was my master."

Thom sat perfectly rigid, searching Linn's face. "And?"

Linn loosened her hold. "A friend on board kicked over the brazier they used to call up Rane. And I jumped overboard." She stroked the animal's head. "A group of these animals saved me."

Thom blinked. "Kjaerdyrer came to save you? They brought you ashore from the *Dark Dragon*?"

Linn nodded. "This fellow is a kjaerdyr?" she asked eagerly. "One of the Great One's special animals, the ones told about in the Lysetome?"

"Yes," Thom replied. "And it seems as though he means to keep you. His friend trotted off as soon as I opened the door of the blind this morning." He leaned forward and tickled the kjaerdyr's ears. "What are you going to call this little one?"

"Name him! Do you really think he'll stay with me?"

Thom nodded. "Kjaerdyrer don't make attachments lightly, and they don't normally have anything to do with people. But don't get the idea that he's *yours*. I think it tends to be the other way around."

Linn brought the kjaerdyr's blunt face level with her own. "I think I'll call him Faerin. Because it was a fair day when he saved me from the sea!"

Faerin chirruped with satisfaction.

Thom held up two fingers. "Second question. Why did the captain of the *Dark Dragon* think that you were this Hidden Arrow? What farsight do you mean?"

Linn wrapped Faerin's well-muscled length around her neck. Holding out her right hand, palm up, she explained. "He said I had a lysemark. I don't know anything about the farsight. He said it was from Rane."

Thom examined her wound, tracing it with a forefinger. Linn flinched. "Yes, I can see why he thought this might be a lysemark," he muttered under his breath. He closed her hand into a fist and let it go, holding up three fingers as he did so. "Third question. Did the kjaerdyrer lead you to me, or did you just stumble in my direction yesterday?"

His gaze searched her, and again that expression she couldn't read flitted across Thom's face. Almost as though he knew something about her. *How much should I tell him?*

"Well," she began slowly, "the boar chased me to your tree. Before that, the kjaerdyrer and I were walking east from the beach."

"But why east, and not west or north?" Thom pressed.

Linn gazed at him. *Can I trust him?* He had one thing

in his favor: he had no Ranite tattoo. And he hadn't taken her Lysetome. Linn drummed her fingers on her knee. "I followed a path that went to the east."

"There are no paths from the shore." He said it quickly, sharply.

"I know. This was a—a *special* path. It appeared before me and then disappeared behind me. The kjaerdyr thought it right to follow—he butted me with his head," she added a bit defensively.

Thom leaned back and stretched his legs out on the blind's hard-packed earth floor, his expression replete with satisfaction. He smiled at Linn, who stared blankly back at him.

Then a thought occurred to her. She sat straight up and bent toward her host. "I have a question of my own now," she said, holding out her right palm. "How do you know this looks like a lysemark?"

"Because," Thom replied, "I *am* a lyse."

Ten

Linn's mouth fell open. Thom remained as he was for a bit, whistling lightly and gazing up at the smoke hole above his head. Finally he turned to Linn and smiled.

"Surprised? You'll have to start getting used to the way the Great One tends to do things. Always very surprising." He got to his feet and held out a hand, pulling Linn up. "And now, I think we will journey together, you and I."

Linn pulled her hand back and held it protectively close to her body. "How do I know you're a lyse?" she asked suspiciously. "Let me see your lysemark."

"Oh, no, that wouldn't do at all," he responded, pulling on a pair of dark brown gloves. "I'm afraid you'll just have to take my word for it."

Linn thrust her chin out and glared at him. Why

should she trust him when he obviously didn't trust her? *But what choice do I have?* "All right. For now. But where will we go?"

"Well, I'd like to go home. To the City of Trees."

The room spun around for a moment. Linn put her hand to a wall, and the movement stopped. "The City of Trees? Here, in Northain? And more lysefolk?"

"Sixty of us, more or less. Some are traveling, as I am." Thom busied himself loading a pack with various items. "But depend upon it, they'll be interested in you, all right. In fact, they'll be interested in *everything* about you."

Linn squirmed at the thought of sixty people examining her. She twisted her fingers. Should she tell him everything? What if he wasn't a lyse?

But what if he is one? Linn touched his shoulder.

"Before we leave, I have to tell you something important—something you don't know. The captain of the *Dark Dragon* is looking for you—for the lysefolk. To destroy you and the City. My real father hoped I might have a lysegift myself. It was his dream for me." She stared down at the earthen floor, her face burning with embarrassment. "When Tarkin made all this fuss about my wound and the farsight, I wondered. Do *you* think . . . ?"

Thom hoisted the pack onto his back in one quick, spare motion. "That's why I want to leave. Now. If what you say is true, then we haven't any time to spare."

He pushed a bedroll and a second, smaller pack into her arms before slipping from the blind.

Thom walked quickly, making little noise. "I'm as loud as that boar, next to him," Linn grumbled to herself. Her legs felt stiff and unwieldy. To top it off, Faerin lay draped across her shoulders, his short, stubby legs dangling over her chest.

After a mile or so, Linn fell behind. It wasn't just because she was stiff and tired. A shadowy fear fluttered inside her. *Someone is watching us, following every step we take.* Her shoulders twitched periodically, and she kept glancing up into the trees.

Finally, Thom looked back. Without a word he retraced his steps and tried to take Faerin from her. It took some persuasion, but the animal eventually transferred his bulk to Thom's shoulders. After that, the trio moved a bit more quickly.

Camp that night was a scratch affair. "I think we'll skip the fire," Thom said, hands on his hips. He took a long look around the site he'd chosen. "There's something . . . something doesn't seem . . ." He trailed off, his eyes staring into the distance, his body tense.

"Do you hear something?" Linn's voice was low.

"Why? Do you?"

"No, I don't *hear* anything." She shivered. "But I *feel* something. Something's wrong. I'm scared."

Thom crouched next to Linn where she sat on a flat rock. "That settles it. We won't light a fire. We don't want to attract anything here in the middle of nowhere. Let's just eat and sleep."

The pair chewed some strips of dried meat and washed them down with warm water from Thom's leather waterskin. Then Linn curled up in her bedroll, Faerin nestled around her head.

"Aren't you going to sleep, Thom?"

He huddled atop a large boulder a few feet beyond her legs, his figure outlined against the night sky. "I'll sleep later. Right now I want to think. Go to sleep. I'll wake you right before dawn."

Despite Thom's admonition, Linn lay awake for a very long time. She must have dozed in the end, though, because a pounding headache woke her up. Her jaw was locked, teeth clenched tightly together. She worked her muscles loose, stretching her mouth open with care to yawn.

Crick. Cra-ik. Crick crick. Linn's head jerked toward the sound. *Cleek, cleek.* Maybe it was some kind of bird, and yet . . . *Cree-ek.*

She turned back toward the rock Thom had been sitting on earlier. "Thom—" No one sat on the rock now. She turned full-circle. The campsite was utterly silent and completely empty.

Faerin! Where was he? "*Whee-weet. Whee-weet.*" Linn pursed her lips and whistled softly. "Faerin, Faerin." No response.

She stood still, straining to hear or see *something.*

Finally, a movement caught her eye. Deep in the gloom, off to the left of the rock, crouched a shadow darker than any shadow could be. With barely discernible movement, it crept toward her, hunched and black, and there was something about it, something—

Blink. Something blinked at her. Something red, something glowing and red and round came at her out of the predawn shadows, and it came on like a running panther until she turned and ran for the other side of the woods and—

"Ooof!" She hit something hard and landed flat on her bottom. Dizzily she reached out to touch the thing before her. A tree. Just a tree.

"Sssssss." Faerin stood next to her, but she almost didn't recognize him. His fur stood straight up, making him appear twice as large as normal. He ignored her, glaring at something in the woods behind her. His teeth gleamed white and strong as his mouth opened again. *"Hissssssss."*

"Linn." She looked up. Thom loomed over her, expressionless and still. "Get up. What are you doing awake?"

She scrambled to her feet, then clutched at him as her legs turned to mush. "Did you see that thing over there?" She pointed with a trembling forefinger, and sweat curled around her upper lip. "There, there!" she insisted when Thom's face remained blank.

"Calm down. I don't see anything. Nothing's there.

Lie down again. You've got an hour or so before we have to get moving. Lie down and go back to sleep."

Linn obeyed him, wrapping her bedroll around her shaking body. "Where were you? Where did you go?"

"Nowhere. I just made a round of the woods. I thought I heard a noise, but it was nothing. Now sleep."

"I heard something too. I saw something! It chased me; it came after me! Didn't you see it?"

Thom glanced over by the rock again. "I doubt you saw anything, Linn. I didn't. Nothing was there. I'm trained to track birds, and believe me, my hearing is far better than yours. I would have noticed if something were there. I would have seen its prints or heard its steps. There was nothing."

A tear sneaked down Linn's cheek. "It was there. It was. I saw it."

Thom shook his head and moved back to his perch atop the rock.

"It was there, wasn't it?" Linn whispered into her blanket. Another tear dropped onto her hand. She couldn't stop shaking.

Then something warm crept into her bedroll, wiggling into place against her. "Taerin!"

"*Chi-ir, chi-ir.*" He made a comforting sound in the back of his throat.

Linn rolled over and hugged him. His body felt warm, but tense and hard, too. His fur stood as stiff against her hands as a hedgehog's spines. "You believe me, don't you? You saw something! I heard you hiss at that thing!" She glanced over at Thom's shadow on the rock. "Did he see something, boy? Or are we on our own?"

"*Hissssss.*"

Eleven

The path Thom took twisted its way up steep hills. "We have to cross a line of foothills that separates us from the Farness River. The river leads toward the City." His voice drifted down to her as he heaved himself over a rocky ledge. "This"—he gestured with a hand—"is a hidden pass known only to the lysefolk—at least I *think* only the lysefolk know of it.

"I doubt very much that anyone else would have any reason to travel beyond these mountains," he panted. "As far as they know, there's nothing north of them except wilderness and wasteland. Just as there's nothing east of the Farness. At least nothing that they know anything about."

"So no one comes near the City?"

"We get an occasional wanderer," Thom replied, picking his way between two flinty boulders. "Since they don't know it's there, they never come too near."

"Can't they see it?"

Thom stopped and looked back at her. "No more than you can see my lysemark," he said, holding up his gloved hand.

"Why?" she shot back, nettled.

Thom said nothing—just gave Linn that long, considering look, as though he knew something she did not. The hackles on the back of her neck rose. She lifted her chin. Thom grinned and resumed his climb. Linn scowled and followed.

They made it over the narrow band of foothills and followed the Farness for half a day. They ate cheese and salty flatbread at midday, perched on a rock overlooking the river. Then they trudged on above the stony bank until they came to a place where the river narrowed and shot wildly through its rock-bound channel. Linn's eyes widened as Thom climbed down to stand right next to the churning water.

He turned and looked up at her, his face calm. "We cross here," he shouted.

"How in the Great One's name—" Linn's throat closed up, choking off her response. Since it was useless to argue at a distance, she climbed down to stand beside him. Faerin sported in the spurts of water thrown up as the river dashed against hidden rocks.

"How can we cross here?" Linn, too, had to shout above the noise of the water. "We'll be swept away."

Thom cupped his hands around his mouth and

spoke quietly into her ear. "At least it's fairly shallow and narrow. It's worse further on. The Farness is a wild river. It never rests. Don't worry—you'll make it. You made it through the Midwaters, didn't you?" He pointed to a nearby willow, its roots curled tenaciously around the boulders lining the riverbank. "See that line tied to the tree? It will guide us across."

Linn squinted and could just make out a thin, gray rope, shadow-light in the sun. It stretched from the trunk of the tree right across the river to a second tree on the opposite bank. She swallowed hard. *At least it's not the Midwaters!*

Thom scooped up Faerin and wrapped him around his neck. Then he balanced atop a broad, flat boulder and grabbed the line that stretched just above his shoulders. Carefully, his gloved hands sliding easily along the gray rope, he moved away from the bank, picking his way on submerged rocks. It wasn't long before the water swirled to his waist.

He turned once, yelling, "Come on!" above the pounding water. With trembling hands, Linn moved forward.

As she reached out for the line, panic overwhelmed her. *I ought to have gloves—I'll lose my grip if the rope tears my wound!* But as soon as she touched the rope, Linn realized that gloves weren't necessary. The line's fibers were as smooth and tight as finely woven linen, not at all like the rough cordage used aboard the *Dark Dragon*. It felt dense and comfortable in her hands. "All right. Now!" She stepped out into the foaming turbulence.

Linn's teeth chattered as the ice-cold water tore through her clothes. Spray slapped her face, drenching her hair with its faintly fishy smell. She shuffled out into the river, feeling her way across the irregular rocks beneath the rapids.

Thom gained the other side and turned to wave her in. "Come on! You're halfway here!"

Snorting water out of her nostrils, she shuffled along on tiptoe to keep her nose above water. The river was up to her earlobes now.

"Aagh!" Her scream ended in a gurgle as she slid under the foam. Her feet swung over her head and thrashed about to find solid ground. *No!* The scream filled her head as the rope slipped from her grasp. *Help me, Great One!*

Suddenly her chest shot up, yanked to the surface of the water. She pressed her hand to her stomach. Those threads—those threads she'd felt on the beach, on Laefe! *They're lifting me—*

"Huuuuuh!" Linn's head pushed out of the water, and she sucked in breath after sweet breath. The rope bobbed above her head, and she stretched, fingers scrabbling, to take a firm grip with one hand, then the other. With a roaring in her ears and the threads pulling and pulsing in her chest, she shuffled across and reached the other side of the river.

"Linn!" Thom splashed over and heaved her up out of the water. "Are you all right? What happened?"

He put her down, and she lay on the rocky bank gasping for air, feeling to make sure the Lysetome was still secure beneath her tunic. Water streamed from her hair and clothes, and her head seemed to float above her body. Everything looked blurry and unfocused. "Who made that rope? Don't tell me it was a lyse!"

Thom grinned. "How did you guess? Liam the Weaver made it. And he told the rest of us he wove confidence into its core."

"Ha! He should have made a bridge instead!"

"*Chirr, chirrup?*" Faerin nosed her face, and Linn grabbed him and held him tight. She sat up, giggling with relief, and looked across the river to where Liam's rope was tied to the willow. Her body stiffened, and she clutched Faerin so hard he squeaked.

"What's that?" She pointed and tottered to her feet. "What's that thing?"

Thom shaded his eyes with his hand. "Where?"

"There, at the foot of the tree the rope is tied to. It's a shadow, a silver shadow. Can't you see it?"

"I don't see anything. Are you sure, or is this another phantom?"

"Yes! I'm sure! I can see right through it—the trees behind it look distorted and strange—but it's there!" Slowly, the thing melted into the shadow of the willow until it disappeared. "There! It's gone now!"

Thom scratched his head and continued to stare. "There's a rumor the lysefolk heard . . . I didn't want to tell you, but . . . they believe that Rane has gained a new skill. Since he's not a true god, he can't be everywhere at once. But a few, trustworthy Truens reported that now, with the destruction of so many of the skjolder, Rane can appear at will, without being called up by the Ranites. And if he has been alerted that you might be this Hidden Arrow he fears . . . well." Thom shrugged. "He might have found a way to follow you."

Linn's stomach dropped. "Do you think that's possible? That the shadow I saw is Rane?"

Thom shrugged again. "How can I know? I didn't see it. And this new power is just speculation. None of the lysefolk has seen Rane appear. And the Truens have only heard about it from others. But I have a feeling we made it across the Farness just in time." He looked across to the other bank, then back at Linn. "I think we'd better keep going." He lifted Faerin and drew Linn into an evergreen forest.

As they trudged on, the sky clouded over. Linn shivered in her wet clothes—wetness didn't seem to bother Thom—and her wounded hand throbbed with feverish pain. When they finally stopped to make camp, Thom built a roaring fire and hung their blankets as close to it as possible. Luckily, he'd wrapped the food in oilskin, so it was still edible. After their meal, he washed out her wound and wrapped a plain strip of linen loosely around it, then gave her a swallow of something for the pain. It burned and tasted of honey.

"Now I'll show you how to make up a bed. You want it close to the fire—but not too close. Make a deep pile of evergreen needles, cover that with your cloak—see, it's dry now—and make a hollow in the center." He kneaded the pile. "Then cover yourself with your blanket and you're set for the night."

She nestled into the pile and pulled her blanket over her; Faerin curled around her head. His warmth relaxed her whole body, and the pain in her hand lessened. She stretched it protectively across her ribs. Now that she was still, the pulling threads resumed their tension, gently tugging instead of yanking. *As though they're protecting me*, she thought as a yawn nearly split her face in two. *I hope I'll be able to sleep tonight.*

"Linnet." Thom interrupted her thoughts, his gaze meeting hers across the fire. "Why do you hold your hand over your ribs like that?"

Linn's face burned for a moment, and she turned away. Her eyes crept back to his rough face. His eyes were sharp and watchful, and that wondering look was back. . . . Well, she wondered about some things herself—these threads, for instance.

"I have a feeling right here." She pointed. "It, well, *pulls* on me, as if a thousand threads were—oh, I don't know!" Linn stopped as Thom smiled. She peered at him suspiciously, wondering if he was laughing at her.

He motioned for her to continue. "I felt it first when I saw the path on Laefe. And I feel it every time the path appears. When I fell in the river, it pulled me up. And now, and now . . ." His smile widened. She threw up her hands. "Oh, I can't explain it!" She lay back, embarrassed.

Thom came over to sit between Linn and the fire. Without a word, he stretched out his hand in the air above her ribs.

It was as though lightning struck her. A rush of power surged into her body, through her ribs and right into Thom's hand. She tried to roll away but couldn't. She lay pinned to the ground, chest heaving, as though she'd run all the way from Sand.

Thom nodded and withdrew his hand. He got up and moved back across the fire, settling into his bedroll as if nothing had happened.

"What was that?" she croaked.

"The lysetett. It's a marker—a bit like a Ranite's tattoo. It's one of the signs that let us know if a claimant really is a lyse. I wondered if you felt it. My only question now is, why do you feel it when your gift operates? It doesn't behave that way with the sixty."

Linn lay stunned. "Do you think this means I truly *am* a lyse?"

Thom yawned and stretched before replying. "That is what I brought you along to find out." Then he rolled over.

Linn sat up and stared at his blanketed back. "That's it? That's all you're going to say?"

"That's all for now. Go to sleep! We have a long tramp tomorrow if we're to get to the City the day after." He settled himself with an annoyed grunt.

Linn lay back down, and Faerin resumed his position around her head. Why wouldn't Thom commit himself? Surely it was evident to him! Either she was a lyse or she wasn't! Didn't he want her to know?

She rolled over, pounding the fir needles into a more comfortable shape. Suddenly she stopped, fist poised midthump. A picture of him that first night in the forest, looming over her and dismissing her fears, rose in her mind. An uneasy feeling came over her.

What if Thom wasn't a lyse? She hadn't seen his lyse-mark with her own eyes, had she? Just because he claimed to know about the lysefolk didn't make him one. And this lysetett—how was it that she'd never read of it in the Lysetome? Was he really taking her to the City of Trees?

Or was this another Ranite plot to stop the Hidden Arrow?

Twelve

"Here we are, home at last." Thom jumped from the edge of the dense forest onto the narrow beach below. Before him stretched a huge body of water, glittering in the midday sun. "You'd think it was a giant lake, wouldn't you? But it's not—it's an inlet connected by a very narrow channel to the Midwaters. We call it Trebay."

Linn scrambled down onto the sand. Faerin roused briefly from his sleepy perch across her shoulders, jarred by her sudden movement. The lysetett—if it was indeed that—pulsed steadily in her chest, a second heartbeat.

"But where is the City? All I see is water and a lot of trees and that mist rising off the surface over there." She pointed to a distant cloudiness that sat lightly on the moving water.

Thom looked down at her, that unreadable expression on his face once more. "That *is* the City over there," he drawled, nodding toward the mist. "That's our destination."

Linn opened her mouth to ask all the questions that immediately sprang to mind, but she snapped it shut. Better to remain guarded. Instead of blurting out her questions, she kept her own face blank. "Ah. I see."

Thom rustled through a thick tangle of bushes on the edge of the water and drew out a skiff. The boat rode high in the water, as light and delicate as one of the autumn leaves that dotted Trebay's surface. Unlike the squared-off shape of Laefe's wooden smallboats, this skiff's leather hull stretched out, long and narrow and flexible, twisting with the water when the waves hit it.

She climbed aboard, grabbing the sides as Faerin jumped from her shoulders straight into the inlet. Then, with a single, easy movement, Thom slid into the boat and began to row out toward the mist.

The skiff sliced through the water, responding easily to Thom's slightest touch. The shore faded swiftly into the distance. As they neared the wall of mist, Thom shipped the oars. He motioned to Linn. "Put your hand in the water. Go on. Feel it."

Linn gazed down into the bay. The water was clear straight to the inlet's bottom. Fish darted among waving plants and over the compact shadow cast by the boat. Faerin shot into view, and he twisted over and over in a joyous spiral, disappearing beneath the skiff. Linn put out one finger to touch the water.

"It's warm! The water's as warm as a bath!"

Thom nodded. "Taste it."

She dipped her cupped hand into the water and gingerly brought it up to sip. Then she took a deep draft. "It's warm, but it's sweet, too!" Water dripped down her chin. "Shouldn't it be salty if this is an inlet?"

Thom nodded. "There's an island out there, in the mist. That's where the City is. The inlet bed is dotted with hundreds of hot springs—all around the island. The steam"—he flourished a hand—"comes from them. And they surround the island with sweet water." He grunted as he bent forward and resumed rowing. "They also protect the City from unfriendly eyes."

The bright autumn world fell behind as, with one powerful stroke, Thom propelled them into a blind world of steam. The skiff, Thom, and Linn's own drab clothes suddenly glowed with color against the white background. Drops of water beaded her hair and face. The silence pressed on her head, as oppressive as the summer sun at midday. Yet despite the warmth Linn shivered, wondering if this really was the way to the City.

Without warning, another stroke thrust the skiff out of the mist. A densely wooded island loomed before them, giant trees stretching up to the sky. Some of them were so massive that a ring of ten men couldn't encircle their trunks.

"It *is* a city of trees," Linn breathed.

Thom threw himself into rowing to the north. "We'll come ashore on the other side of the island," he puffed between strokes.

It took a good part of the early afternoon to row along the north shore. The circle of mist created a vast, unceilinged, yet very private room. *Safe but dangerous, hidden and still exposed*, Linn thought. The lysetett trembled and twisted in her chest.

Finally, the eastern side of the island slid into view. A broad, shallow beach of white sand climbed from the water, forming a perfect hollow for landing the skiff. Thom leaped from the bow, holding it steady while Linn climbed out into the warm water. As he pulled the craft higher up on the beach, she coaxed the reluctant kjaerdyr from the water into her arms. Then she turned for her first glimpse of the City of Trees.

It wasn't a city at all. A small flock of sheep grazed on a distant hillock. To the south, a large natural clearing was divided into smaller gardens. Most of these had been harvested and were already plowed for their winter's rest. Clean clothing danced from one long rope stretched between two poles, while lengths of white cloth lay on a field of grass, bleaching in the sun's rays.

"But where are the lysefolk? Where is the City—all its houses?" Disappointment and renewed suspicion clogged Linn's throat. "You lied to me, didn't you?" she choked out. "We're nowhere near the City!" She backed away from Thom. "And you're not a lyse, are you? *Are you?*"

Thom's face grew still and white. "If you thought I was lying, why did you follow me?"

"Did I have a choice?" she shot back. "I had nothing—no food, no drink, no shelter! What should I have done?"

"I am a lyse," he said, lifting his chin. "The other lysefolk are here. And we don't need houses." A look of disdain—or something close to it—burned in his eyes. "You fancy yourself a lyse? You want to see the other lysefolk? Then prove your gift. Find them yourself."

"What's going on here?" A voice interrupted their argument. Linn whirled around. A tall, stately woman with long silver hair and skin the color of cherrywood stood behind her. She clasped a bundle of golden wheat under her right arm, and a flail for separating chaff from grain hung from her left hand. "Thom, you're back." Her eyes, black like Linn's, seemed to bore through Linn's skin into the very marrow of her bones. The woman's expression was wary. "Who is this with you?"

Thom's eyes flashed. "She says she's a lyse. I found her by my blind on the other side of the Farness." He pointed at Faerin. "That kjaerdyr and one other were with her."

"But I never said I was a lyse." Linn's tone was sulky from embarrassment. "I only said I wondered if I was."

The woman arched one eyebrow. "And are you?"

Linn looked at the ground and shuffled her feet. She held out her hands, pleading. "I don't know. I think I might be. . . . I seem to have a gift."

The tall woman frowned and dropped the wheat and flail on the ground. She stepped forward and picked up Linn's right hand, examining the wounded palm. Thom joined her.

"What do you think, Maren? Could that be a lyse-mark?"

Maren bit her lip, and the wrinkles around her eyes deepened. She glanced at Thom. "Does she have a gift? Is she a lyse, or could she be . . . ? "

Thom shrugged. "That's why I brought her here. We all need to decide together. And since a Gathering has been called and most of the lysefolk are in the City right now, it seemed to me . . ." He trailed off, questioning the older woman with his eyes.

Linn shrank back. "I'm not a prize pig on market day, you know! I'm not here to be judged! And who are you to judge me, anyway? How do I really know you're lysefolk?"

The lysetett reacted then. It stretched out, pulling as far away from her as possible, rebuking her. Panic shot through Linn. *No—don't leave me!* she begged, her wounded hand feeling for the Lysetome under her tunic. *Please forgive me!* The lysetett gave one last tug of correction.

Thom and Maren stood looking at her. Linn could tell from their expressions that they knew exactly what the lysetett had done. Without a word, Maren held out her right hand for Linn to see the palm. In the center, silver against brown, was a lysemark in the shape of a sheaf of wheat.

Again Linn cast her eyes to the ground. "I'm sorry," she mumbled. Her tongue felt thick and clumsy. "You probably are a lyse. I know you must judge my gift, whether it be true or no. You have that right as a lyse."

"No right," Maren replied quietly. "Just the responsibility, whether we want to judge or not." She sighed. "Believe me, girl, I'd far rather not have the judgment." Then she turned back to Thom. "Well, what of it? What is her gift? Which of the dying lysefolk will she replace?"

"That's just it," he replied. "It's not a replacement gift. It's something else, something new. A gift for finding a path."

Maren put her hand to her heart, and her face paled. "Finding a path? Do you know what this might mean?"

Thom nodded, his face a stiff mask. "Yes. I brought her right here when I found her. It could mean everything—or it could mean nothing. But we must make a decision about her now, before it's too late."

Maren looked deep into Linn's eyes again. "Are you ready to meet the lysefolk? Are you ready to enter the City of Trees, girl?"

Linn took one step back and licked her lips nervously. Faerin nuzzled her cheek, giving her a tiny nugget of courage. "All right. I'm ready, I guess."

"Good." Maren swept her arm wide toward the forest. "Then prove your gift now. Find it."

Thirteen

Linn swallowed hard, the nugget of courage shrinking inside her. Then the lysetett returned. It rippled across Linn's skin and gently beckoned her forward. She could almost hear someone standing at her ear, whispering, "Use the gift."

Standing in a patch of sunshine, she closed her eyes and reached deep inside to the spot where the lysetett pulsed with a steady, humming tension. She looked back at Thom and Maren, who stood with inscrutable expressions, then stepped out onto the grass from the sandy beach.

As soon as her foot touched the blades, they bent low to the ground, stretching out before her like a carpet. Maren clutched Thom's arm. "Oh, holy Great One. She does have a gift."

The path drew them deep into the giant forest. Flashes of sunlight pierced the evergreen canopy far overhead. Birds dove before them, and hares darted over the bending grasses that pointed the way. Linn drew in deep breaths of fir-scented air. And the lysetett tugged her on. *Home, home, home.* The grasses sprang upright again as Linn stepped into a large clearing.

Sounds drifted down from high above. The clink of knife on plate and bottle on cup. Low voices murmured overhead, drawing Linn's gaze up.

A stone tower stood before her, a fine-boned white spear thrusting toward the blue sky. Wide stone steps led from the floor of the clearing to a pair of carved oaken doors that opened into the tower itself.

Thom let loose a high-pitched, single-note whistle. Suddenly windows all over the spire popped open, and people of every skin and hair color leaned out to look down on Linn's head.

"Lysefolk?" she asked, staring up.

"Who else?" Thom stepped forward, his eyes focused on the faces above. "Well, here you are at last, Linnet," he murmured in her ear. "What about it? Do you think they'll let a false lyse like me in? And how about a suspicious-minded girl who fancies herself a lyse?" He flashed a mocking little grin.

Her face burned. She looked up into his eyes, pleading. "I'm so sorry. You *are* lysefolk—both of you." She turned to Maren. "Friends?"

Maren nodded and Thom bowed again, taking Linn's wounded hand and planting a kiss on its back. "All is forgiven, all is forgotten. Now let's go inside." He pulled open one of the tower's heavy, ornately carved doors for her. Linn bent down and picked up Faerin. As she brushed by, Thom laid hold of her upper arm. "Courage, Linn!" he told her. She squeezed his hand and entered the tower.

The huge round room they stepped into took up the whole first level. Autumn sunlight streamed through evenly spaced arched windows all around its perimeter. A staircase, curving up the far white wall, led to the tower's second level. Lysefolk—real lysefolk!—scurried down it, no doubt to get a look at her.

The room itself was crammed with tables, chairs, shelves, books, animals, and people. It was the people who held her attention. Most were much, much older than Thom—he was one of the youngest in the room. Some kind of animal—a songbird, a mouse, a squirrel, a sleek fox—accompanied every one. A speckled mountain cat came over to rub against Maren's skirts.

The lysetett exploded in Linn's chest, and she wrapped her arms around her ribs to contain it. The invisible threads stretched taut, vibrating with excitement. She turned to Thom. "Do you feel that? Do they?"

He nodded and smiled sympathetically. "Come on," he whispered. "Let's get this over with." Holding her hand tightly in his, he wove his way through the crowd and led her onto a dais near the room's center.

"Friends!" he cried, his voice formal and commanding. "Friends, gather 'round to hear and judge a matter I will lay before you." Then, as the lysefolk rose and drew near, Thom put his arm around Linn and walked her in a full circle around the platform, halting in the very center. "I found this girl southeast of the City. She is a Truen and has come all the way from Laefe to seek the City and the lysefolk. She believes she has a lysegift."

Linn stared at her toes, wriggling her shoulders in discomfort at this proclamation. Thom ignored her, responding instead to the questions the lysefolk had begun to ask. He held up his hand for silence. "She feels the lysetett. Do you feel it with her?" Several lysefolk gave wary assents. Thom pointed to Faerin. "And her companion is a kjaerdyr, beloved animal of the Great One. A group of them rescued her from the Midwaters."

A dark-headed young man stepped forward. He stroked the light-colored brush of whiskers on his chin. A tiny finch cocked its bright eyes at Linn from its perch atop the man's head.

"Lysetett or no, how can she be one of us? No one among the failing lysefolk has died. We are still sixty; the number of lysefolk is yet complete." Muttering filled the room.

Maren raised her arm to be heard. "Wait, Daern, let the girl speak," she said in a voice that, though low, carried far. "We must know all the facts before we judge." The speckled mountain cat let forth an approving rumble.

"Well said, Maren," Thom agreed. "The girl's name is Linnet of Laefe. The kjaerdyr with her is Faerin." He stepped down and took his place among the lysefolk.

Linn rubbed her hands on her tunic and licked her dry lips. "My farr, his farr, and his grandfarr worshipped the Great One. I inherited their Lysetome." She pulled it from her tunic and held it up. As she did so, she noticed Lysetomes on several of the tables by the dais. "Farr died when I was just four seasons old. My mother—" Linn's mouth twisted, and she stopped to compose herself. "My mother then wed a Ranite."

"No!" A shocked murmur rose from the lysefolk. Maren stared down and shook her head. Linn glanced at Thom, who nodded and made a little palms-out pushing gesture. She continued.

"My stepfather beat me. I put up with that. But then he promised me to a Ranite and told me that I must become Ranite as well. That I could not bear." Another murmur, this time approving. "So I decided to run away and hide somewhere in the mountains on Laefe. But then . . ." She took a deep, steadying breath. "But then a path appeared before me. A path that led me to a ship in Laefe's harbor. It was a path of bending grasses, like a carpet. When I took a step, it rolled out ahead. When I passed by, it disappeared behind me."

Daern stood up, his finch fluttering over and around his head. "What makes you believe this is a lysegift? It's not even hinted at in the Lysetome."

Linn met his look straight on. "There is more. I felt the lysetett for the first time when the path appeared. It helped draw me to the ship. I stowed away with the help of the cabin boy." The memory of Gee's round face gave her a spurt of boldness. "He told me that the Ranites are searching for the City of Trees. They plan to destroy it—and you. When the captain of the ship discovered me in the hold, he called up Rane. Gee, the cabin boy, saved me."

"How?" Maren raised her head, surprised.

"Gee overturned the brazier they used to summon Rane. I jumped overboard. A group of kjaerdyrer saved me, brought me to land. I followed the path again when it appeared, and the lysetett urged me on. The path brought me to Thom."

Daern shot Thom a questioning look. Thom gave one short nod. Daern leaned forward. "But why? Why would these Ranites call on Rane to deal with you, a mere girl?"

Linn shifted uneasily, glancing at Thom. He put out a gloved hand, palm up. Reluctantly, Linn followed suit.

"This is why. They said I had a lysemark, here on my hand." She swallowed the lump rising in her throat. "They said . . . they said I was the Hidden Arrow of Rane's farsight."

The room trembled with silence. Daern shoved forward to get a better look at Linn's hand. But a short, broad lyse with thick white hair and smooth dark skin barred his way. The black squirrel on his shoulder chattered with indignation. "Now, now, age before beauty, young one! Let your elders look first." He squinted down at Linn's palm.

"Hmm. I see why the Ranites thought this might be a lysemark." He touched the wound with a fat but gentle forefinger. Linn winced. "It's fresh. And you got this mark aboard ship?"

"No. I got it on Laefe. From my Ranite stepfather."

Maren exchanged a glance with the broad lyse. "What do you think, Cam? Could it be a lysemark?"

Cam squinted down at the wound again. "Don't know. It certainly doesn't resemble ours." He held out his hand to reveal a silvery star-shaped mark.

The pair stepped aside, and other lysefolk crowded forward to look. Then they retreated, talking among themselves in low, urgent voices. Linn squirmed. "*Chirrup.*" Faerin leaped into her arms and wrapped his comforting length about her shoulders.

A bent, elderly lyse who was missing most of the hair on his pink crown hobbled over to Thom. A white ferret curled around his neck, asleep. He eyed Linn, then patted Thom's back. "Don't you worry. She's a lyse, sure enough."

A faint, gentle smile flitted across Thom's face. "What makes you so sure, Liam?"

The old lyse pursed his lips. Linn drew nearer to hear. "She has the Great One's favor. Have you ever seen a kjaerdyr attach itself to someone before?" He took the Lysetome from Linn, riffling through it until he found the section he wanted. " 'And in the Midwaters the Great One released the kjaerdyr, beloved animal *that loves no one save Him alone,*' " he read, tapping the page with a finger that was flat and broad from years of weaving. "She must be a lyse. Maybe she's more."

Warmth flooded Linn's body. She stepped off the dais and took Liam's hands in hers. A silver wheel shone on the dry pink skin of his right palm. "You're the weaver who made the rope across the Farness?"

The old man's eyes twinkled. "I surely did, young one."

"Thank you," she whispered.

Daern's voice rose above the others, and Linn turned back to hear him. "Can she really be one of us? Would a lysemark appear through a Ranite beating? We all got ours when we bore the white fire of Maer."

Linn tilted her head toward Thom's. "The white fire?" she repeated.

"Each lyse proves his calling by thrusting a hand into a white-hot firepit," he explained. "If it comes out scorched or burned, there is no call. If a lysemark appears, all is well." Linn's eyes widened. The Lysetome didn't say anything about this. Thom's face was serious. "It is a grave thing to claim a place as a lyse."

Maren cut in. "We called this Gathering months ago because we need an urgent answer to our problem. Our strength as lysefolk is waning. Five lie on their deathbeds as we speak. If we don't find a way to renew the skjolder soon, to renew our own power, our numbers will dwindle to fifty-five. It will be the beginning of the end."

"I've been searching the skies for an answer every night," Cam added. "The stars tell of two things: doom for Maether and hope from the west. Our doom is not certain as long as the skies also speak of hope. I believe that hope is Rane's bane, the Hidden Arrow he fears. We know the answer had to be the Hidden Arrow." He nodded at Thom. "We had Thom and Bree and five others posted along the Northain coast watching for the Arrow."

Linn looked at Thom, who blushed. "So you did know about the farsight!" she whispered. "You were looking for someone like me all along!"

Thom nodded. "I saw the path that first day too. Before the boar chased you, I saw you from up in the tree. But I couldn't be sure you were the Arrow. I'm sorry." He looked into her eyes. "All the lysefolk have to make that decision together. Understand?" Linn nodded.

Maren had begun speaking again. "Has fortune been with us? Is the wound in Linnet's hand the sign of Rane's farsight? Have we truly found the Hidden Arrow?"

"Or is this just a trick of Rane's?" Another lyse spoke out.

Daern broke the silence that followed. "We have only one choice. We must test her."

"But how?" Thom asked, glancing sideways at Linn.

"There is a way, a sure way." Daern's voice intensified. "Send her to search for Maer's Lake."

Someone in the back of the tower gasped. Thom grew still. Linn searched his face, puzzled.

Maren pushed her hair back from her forehead. She looked very tired. "Grania failed to find it. Should we send another—especially one untried and young—to search? I thought we had agreed that way was closed."

"What other choice do we have?" Daern persisted. "She says she has a path-finding gift. If she *is* the Arrow and *does* have such a gift, perhaps the Great One sent her to show us where the lake is. If she finds the lake and brings back its water, perhaps she'll return in time to save the failing lysefolk!"

A wave of approval swelled from the group, and Maren looked a trifle less weary. She nodded. "Yes. That is well thought out, Daern. What do the rest of you say?"

Every voice spoke approval, save one. Thom remained silent, his face fixed and tense.

Maren drew Linn up the dais steps, then looked into her eyes. "Do you accept this test, Linnet of Laefe? Will you undertake to prove your gift? The future of Maether may be in your hands."

Fourteen

aerin slipped from her arms. The room grew so quiet that Linn could hear Thom's ragged breathing. It pounded in her ears. She looked over at him, pleading silently for help. But Thom didn't look up. He kept his eyes fixed on his feet. The lysetett ceased completely, and fear rose to fill its place in her chest. She turned back to Cam and Maren.

"Why do I have to prove my gift by leaving the City?" Linn's voice sounded tight and high in her ears. "Isn't there another way? I've waited my whole life to find this City. Don't send me away already. Please let me stay!"

Maren's eyes were sympathetic, but Linn sensed iron behind their black gaze. "I understand," she said patiently. "We all understand. Believe me, this is not a trip we would willingly send anyone on, least of all someone so young. We've already lost one lyse to the quest. The

Great One knows we don't want to lose anyone else, true lyse or no. But we're running out of time."

"You lost a lyse? Who? When?" The fear rose a little higher in Linn's chest.

Maren opened her mouth to answer, but Cam put a restraining hand on her arm. "Best leave that story for Thom to tell—or not," he said. Maren nodded. "But you should know, Linnet, that if we do not get this water, and get it soon, the lysefolk will die out, and all of Maether will perish with them."

"What's so special about this water?" Linn asked. "I know Maer's Lake is the place where the very first lyse met the Great One face-to-face. I've read about that in the Lysetome. But why do you need water from it so badly?"

Daern cut in eagerly. "Maer's Lake is said to be the Great One's dwelling place on Maether. Not that he needs a place to live," he corrected himself hastily, "but it's a place he loves. And from all reports, it's a place Rane hates."

"Why?"

"Isn't that obvious?" Daern's eyes goggled. "Rane hates the Great One, hates the lysefolk, and hates Maether. Surely he'd hate this place, Maether's most sacred spot!"

Cam waved Daern aside. "The important point is this, Linnet. Over the last twenty years, the skjolder— the strong places—have been destroyed, one by one.

They were the sentinels that held Rane at bay." He shook his head. "It's terrible. The skjolder may look like trees, but they are living, thinking beings like us. They draw the blessing of the golden water on which Maether floats up through their deep roots and then shed it abroad through their branches."

Cam swallowed and an expression of pain flitted across his face. "The Ranites found a way to harness the lesser demons. They called them up as wraiths and formed them into jackals in order to sniff out the whereabouts of the skjolder. When the wraiths found the strong places, the Ranites surrounded the skjolder with fire and burned them alive until only stumps were left. They couldn't escape and their roots withered away, no longer able to take up the water. And now only three remain, and as they dwindle, our powers as lysefolk wane. Most of us are very old. What if we die and none rise up to take our places?"

Linn felt sick, but Thom looked grim. Several lyse-folk covered their faces.

Liam hobbled over and interjected, "Rane would win and that would be the end of Maether. He would destroy it, just as he destroys everything that comes under his dominion. But the lake water can turn the tide."

"How?" Linn asked.

"Lend me your Lysetome again, daughter." Liam took the worn volume in his gnarled hands. "Look. 'Maer saw the lake glittering like gold in the sun.

Its water was pure and holy, the best on Maether, because it contained the life of the Great One.' You know that Maether is like the cream on a pail of milk. It floats atop the sacred water of the Great One. In certain places, near the skjolder and at Maer's Lake, the water pushes through into Maether. That water is pure and unsullied." Liam smiled at Linn. "It is liquid holiness."

"And if the lysefolk can obtain some of the water from Maer's Lake, we can use it to restore the destroyed skjolder. Then we can fight to keep Maether alive and defeat Rane." This time it was Thom who spoke. He looked into Linn's eyes for a long moment, his face still unreadable.

Linn drew a shaky breath. "Now I understand a little. If I am a lyse and do have a path-finding gift, I am the logical choice to undertake this quest."

Maren nodded. "Yes. It will serve two purposes, as Daern said. It will prove your gift and may save the lysefolk and the skjolder. But no matter how great our need, the choice is yours alone."

"Could Thom come with me?"

Liam shook his head. "It's your test, not his, daughter. You must go without a lyse, but you may take Faerin."

Linn squeezed her eyes shut, trying to clear her mind and concentrate. But questions chased around and around in her head. *Should I go or not? I'm not strong or brave—why does it have to be me? What if I don't have a gift? What will happen to me?*

Her thoughts ran back to Farr. What would he advise her to do? She pushed the question away. *I have to decide for myself now. It's my test, my life.*

She opened her eyes. "How can I decide?" she asked Maren. "It took everything in me to make it to the City. And now . . ." A sob caught in her throat.

Liam tottered forward and patted Linn's arm. "Now, daughter, our cause is urgent, yes. But the least we can do is let you sleep on it and decide in the morning. All right?"

Linn gave him a grateful smile. Maren took Linn's wounded hand in hers and placed it very gently in Thom's gloved one. "Here, Thom. Take her, feed her, let her rest for tonight. Tomorrow is soon enough for a decision, but tomorrow it must be made."

Slowly Thom's fingers tightened around Linn's, and without looking at her, he waded through the lysefolk, leading her up the winding staircase to the floors above.

At the top of the staircase, almost at the pinnacle of the tower, Thom opened a thick, walnut-paneled door and motioned for Linn to enter. The room reminded her of a nest, its walls feathered with tapestries of woodland scenes. A woven rush mat covered the floor. Shelves stretching to the ceiling displayed a careful collection of feathers, eggs, nests, and drawings of a huge variety of birds.

Despite the autumn chill, the window stood open. Through it knifed the call of a hawk gliding on the night wind. *"Cew-ew!"* With a rush of feathers, the bird seized a perch fixed just outside the window. Linn jumped back clumsily. The hawk shot her a keen look, then hopped onto the sill and into the room. With a glad croak, it swooped over to land on Thom's shoulder, picking gently at the lyse's hair with its beak. Thom reached up to caress the golden-brown neck.

"How I've missed you, Serena," he murmured. His eyes closed and his breathing deepened as he drew in the hawk's strength.

When his eyes opened again, his stoniness seemed to have lessened a bit. He still carefully avoided looking in Linn's direction, his shoulders hunched and set. *Just like mine before one of Domm's beatings,* Linn thought uneasily. *Why?*

She perched on a tall stool, nervously twirling the end of her plait. "I'll be back in a moment," Thom said abruptly, escaping through the door and down the stairs.

Serena settled atop a shelf and preened, darting glances at Linn. To avoid the bird's looks, Linn wandered around the room, picking up a hollow egg here, a tail feather there. A worktable stood near the room's large window. Linn bent over the thick yellow paper pinned to its surface. A painting was in progress: a small brown linnet bird, every feather exquisitely detailed.

Finally the door opened and Thom entered, carrying a wooden tray filled with fresh food. He placed it on the trunk at the foot of his bedstead and drew up two three-legged oak stools. "Come on," he told her. "Might as well eat."

Even though the fresh meat and bread smelled delicious after the dried food she'd been eating, Linn only picked at the meal, letting Faerin consume most of her portion. Thom ate doggedly, as though every mouthful were bitter medicine that had to be choked down somehow. Eventually he laid aside his knife, wiped his mouth on his sleeve, and sank back against the foot of the bed frame.

"What's the plan?" Linn asked, watching his chest rise with quick, shallow breaths. It was a stupid question, but she had to say something to break the silence.

Thom finally met her gaze, looking up at her from his prone position. "Didn't you hear Maren? You have to choose by tomorrow." His abrupt tone felt like a slap.

Linn caught her lower lip between her teeth, biting back the anxiety and anger that wanted to leap out. "Will you help me decide what to do?"

"No. It's your choice, not mine." He bent his head, deliberately not meeting Linn's eyes.

"Thom?" She twisted her fingers in her lap during the silence that followed. "What's wrong with you?" she asked. "Why won't you talk to me? What's the matter?"

Thom's head sank lower. His shoulders stayed rigid

and hunched. Serena ruffled her feathers and stretched out her neck. She looked both bigger and more vulnerable, as though she weren't quite full-grown.

"You want to know what the matter is, Linnet?" Thom asked. "I'll tell you later, after you turn the test down. Or if you do decide to go, I'll tell you when you get back."

"That's no answer!" Linn sprang from her stool and grabbed his arm. "I don't know the first thing about finding this lake. I've waited all my life to find the City of Trees, and now they're asking me to leave immediately." *And you can't come with me!* The sentence echoed in her head.

Thom did look at her then, and his gray eyes were compassionate. But his manner remained distant. He sat her back down on the stool.

"Look, we don't have much time." He covered his face with his hands. "We need you—we need your gift badly. You're our only hope of finding Maer's Lake."

"Why haven't you looked before this?" she asked softly.

Thom's voice was muffled and bitter. "Oh, we have, believe me. Remember what Maren said? We sent Grania to search for the lake two years ago. She never returned. The Great One sent Cam a dream, showed him that Grania was dead and who was to take her place. Then he went off to find Daern. After that we agreed that no one else would search for the lake. It was too

dangerous. We couldn't take the chance of losing another lyse."

"Why didn't you send Serena or have the lyse who is
the master of animals send a wolf or mountain cat to
find the lake?"

"No. We couldn't. Our powers have weakened too
much." He let his hands drop and looked at Linn, his
face red with shame. "I'm reduced to *painting* birds. I
can't call the ones I haven't tamed anymore. Daern is the
master of animals now, and his power is so weak that
only his finch responds regularly to his call. That's why
he's so eager to send you off on this quest. Even Cam,
the master of the stars for over fifty years, has difficulty
reading them. Now he can only see something tremen-
dous, like the destruction of Maether."

An unpleasant thought occurred to Linn. "Does
Rane know where Maer's Lake is? Could he destroy it
before a lyse finds it?"

"The only way he can find either the lake or this City
is by possessing a lyse or following one," Thom said
soberly. "Rane is a demon, a spirit." His mouth twisted
in a grimace. "He usually waits for willing vessels to call
him up. Then he wreaks whatever havoc he can through
them. But now, if the rumors are true and he can appear
at will, who knows?"

Linn trembled, remembering the *Dark Dragon* and the
smell of Rane's breath drifting down on her. And what
of that shadow on the bank of the Farness, and that red

thing that chased her in the woods? Thom got to his feet slowly and heavily, then stood looking down on Linn's head.

"I suspect that's what happened to Grania. Rane found her and followed her. She chose death rather than betray the City or the lake." Thom paused, leaning forward with his hands on the bed. His head bent as though it pained him to hold it upright. "I know it's un-usual—most lysefolk dedicate themselves only to serv-ing the Great One. But Grania was my betrothed. She chose to pursue the hope the lake offered. But she failed. And now you might follow her."

Linn turned her head and looked out the window into the dark sky. The mist surrounding the island gave the night a pearly color. The breeze that blew in the window felt cold on her face. She closed her eyes, and two tears squeezed through her lashes and ran down her cheeks.

When she opened her eyes she found herself looking deep into Thom's gray ones. She'd forgotten how qui-etly he could move. Slowly he lifted Linn's right hand and opened her palm. He gently kissed the wound on her hand and closed her fist over it.

Then he left Linn alone with her decision.

Fifteen

Linn's head felt as if someone had filled it with sludge. Her room was cold and filled with mist. She'd forgotten to shut the window, and the cries of a hawk—probably Serena—had awakened her. Gritty-eyed, she got out of bed, sluggishly pulling on her leggings, shirt, and tunic in the early dawn light, almost forgetting to slip her Lysetome inside.

Sleep had not come easily to Linn the night before. Her head had overflowed with new knowledge of the lysefolk, Rane, Maether, and even herself. *Was* she this Arrow? Did she have the guts to go alone in search of Maer's Lake? And what if Rane followed her on this quest? Would she end up like Grania, sacrificing herself in the wilderness for a vain hope?

Faerin slept on, tucked far beneath the warm bedclothes in a snoring ring of fur. Linn decided against waking him and went down to search for food by herself.

Only a few lysefolk sat in the big room at the bottom of the staircase. They were huddled together at a single table, discussing something in low voices. *Probably me,* Linn thought bleakly when they stopped talking at the sight of her. One of the lysefolk got up and walked over, hand outstretched in welcome. Linn saw a flash of her lysemark, a curling snake.

"Linnet, good morning," the lyse said, tossing one of her two plaits over her shoulder. She was a big, raw-looking woman with hair the orangey color of ripe squash, and bright blue eyes. "My name is Runa. Please excuse my dress." She indicated her stained white shift. "I just spent the night watching one of the failing lysefolk, and I haven't had time to clean up yet. I was too hungry to wait for food any longer!" She laughed, opening her mouth wide and flashing big white teeth. "But I'll wager you're as famished as I was. Come and join us at mornmeal, please."

She brought Linn to the table where the other lysefolk sat, placing her right in the middle between two old women who stared at her with undisguised interest. Runa went over to a sideboard, loaded up a plate and bowl, and brought them back to Linn. Then she sat across from her with a thump.

Despite her lethargy, Linn ate with good appetite. Porridge with nuts, honey, and cream slid down her throat easily, filling her belly as it hadn't been filled since Thom's blind. She finished off two slabs of new-made bread with curds, then drank the warm tea Runa poured for her. The tea revived her, and she faced the curious lysefolk in a stronger frame of mind.

Runa introduced the others around the table. "This is Kenna; she's the mistress of brewing. And here's Jente; she deals with weather-lore. Berl is our sea master and Tirran our mapmaker." Linn shook hands all around. Runa pressed a rough-looking hand to her own chest. "I am the lyse of healing, which explains why I was up all night." The others chuckled as if at an old, often-told joke.

"Well, have you decided yet?" Kenna asked Linn abruptly. She had a flat, expressionless voice that made her question sound insulting. Linn gave her a surprised look. But on second glance, she could see that the old lyse was simply curious.

Tirran laughed and laid a hand on Linn's wounded one. "Don't mind Kenna, Linn. She knows that the shortest path to what you want is a straight one."

Linn smiled. "I'm not offended. I was up half the night worrying. How can I decide? Maren spoke of my youth last night. She was right. I'm not sure what I should do."

The lysefolk exchanged glances. Berl, a squat man with steel-gray hair and skin the texture of driftwood, cleared his throat. "We've all agreed. It's best not to try to influence you. But if you have any questions, we'll answer them as best we may." The others nodded.

"I do have some questions." Linn played with her plait. "How do all the lysefolk come to be here right now? What is this Gathering I heard Liam speak of last night?"

Jente spoke in a quick, light voice. "We've all been here about two months. It's rare that all sixty are together at once in the City. In fact, four of us are still out watching for the Arrow, as Thom was. Of course Cam, our farseer, is almost always here, unless he's sent on a special mission." Her expression darkened. "When Grania died, the Great One came to him in a dream and showed him where to find Daern. He was gone for three months."

"Where do you usually live, then?" Linn asked.

"Why, I travel all over Maether, tracking the weather as best I might." She smiled. "It's not an easy job, but it's always interesting."

"What do you do? How does your weather-gift operate?"

"Oh, that! I must speak to the winds when they blow off-course or threaten to become too troublesome. I weave my spells and unleash the spring rains and make sure the summers don't become too dry. When I was first brought to the City, I spent many weeks poring over the notes and maps of the previous weather-lyse. I had to learn Maer's tongue so I could speak the spells rightly." She laughed. "Now I don't even have to think about the words anymore. They're my true language now, the one I think in most of the time."

Linn looked over at the two men. "And where do you dwell when you're not in the City?"

Tirran brushed his white hair back from his forehead with a hand spotted from age. "I travel, like Jente and Berl. How else can I map Maether? I have a form of farsight that comes to me in dreams and sometimes helps me see a coastline as a bird would. But usually I map a land by traveling it and then pass that knowledge on to shipwrights and sea captains. They never know the maps come from a lyse." He grinned.

Berl grunted. "I also learned Maer's language to say my spells rightly. I sail the seas in my skiff, tracking their moods and quirks." He rubbed his fingers together. "I've got salt water in my veins, girl. Sometimes I can sense what the sea will do next by the feel of the blood coursing through my body. Maybe that's a kind of farsight. Who knows? But I do know that were I to die and none replace me, the seas would rise up against the land and throw all of Maether into their depths."

Linn shuddered, then turned to Kenna. "And you?"

"I stay put in the City most of the year, but when the snows cease, I load my mule with the fruits of my labors and travel to Sand for spring market." Kenna's brown eyes sparkled. "I sell my brew to travelers from all over Maether, giving them hints of how I managed to make such a delicious drink." She smacked her lips, and the others laughed. "None of them, Ranite or common, suspects they take a lyse-brew back to bless their towns and homes. The spells I speak over my bottles are homely, but they do their work well."

"But you asked how we all come to be here at once," Runa reminded Linn. "Cam called a Gathering through the lysetett." Linn looked puzzled. "Oh, once you're confirmed as a lyse"—here the other lysefolk shifted uncomfortably—"you'll learn to ignite the lysetett and use it for various purposes. Not that you can ever quite control it, but it does have its uses." She patted her rib cage.

"Why did Cam call the Gathering?"

"He is our master of stars. He saw Maether's doom and the bane of Rane in the stars. And of course, five of the oldest lysefolk were dying. The Great One hadn't revealed the new lysefolk in a dream to anyone. Once Cam read the sky-signs, he grew very worried. He brought us together so we could beseech the Great One's aid and guidance. We were on the verge of giving up hope when you showed up with Thom." Runa tapped her fingers on the tabletop and looked at Linn from under her lashes.

Linn grew very still. She knew the lysefolk at the table longed for her to take up the quest and bring back the sacred water. Their lives and lyselore depended on it, as did the future of Maether. But Linn sensed something hard and determined in her heart, something that did not want to make the sacrifice they asked. The very pressure of the deadline they'd imposed made this thing dig in its heels to keep her from deciding.

Despising her own selfishness but unable to overcome it, Linn cast about for a different subject of conversation. "Runa, you haven't told me how your gift works. How does it heal?"

Runa eyed Linn with disappointment she couldn't hide. "Come. It's easier to show how my gift works than to explain it." She pushed back her chair with a screech of wood against wood and walked across the rush-strewn floor to the oak doors.

Linn hurried after her. Runa's stride was longer than Thom's, and even though she hadn't slept the night before, she kept a brisk pace. Linn was panting by the time they reached their destination.

It was a huge tree, hollowed out into a one-room dwelling. Runa had to duck to enter by the south-facing door. A stale scent that Linn had smelled at her grandparents' deathbeds stole into her nostrils. She backed away, then, ashamed, came forward into the room again. Ten bedsteads lined the circular room, five of them occupied by lysefolk. Another lyse stood in front of a stone fireplace. She was carefully crushing herbs into a pot of steaming water and murmuring words in a language Linn had never heard before. She finished her task before turning to Linn and Runa.

Her voice was quiet when she spoke. "Linnet, I am Eavan." She held out her hand. Linn took it, and when she withdrew her own hand from the lyse's grasp, she thought the scent of lavender came with it. "Maybe Runa has told you. I am the lyse of herb lore."

"No, she hadn't told me." Linn crossed her arms in front of her, pressing the Lysetome into her chest. "She brought me in to see how her gift works."

"Ah, that is good," Eavan replied. "We often work together, Runa and I. Together we can ease the pain of passing, and sometimes prevent it. But not this time, I fear." She shook her gray head and laid a hand on Runa's shoulder. "It is good you've come back. Berke is worse. The pain even attacks him in his sleep now."

Runa beckoned for Linn to stand at the end of one of the bedsteads, while she and Eavan took a place on either side. The lyse who lay in the bed was almost as white as the bedclothes. His breathing was shallow and rapid, and he picked sporadically at the blanket. Deep lines of pain traced their paths across his forehead, between his eyes, and down each side of his mouth. His wrinkled skin was paper-thin, folded across delicate bones. Linn could clearly see the knotted veins beneath it.

The two lysefolk joined hands over the bedstead and began to chant in the language Eavan had been using over the pot. Linn folded her hands and lowered her eyes but didn't close them. Instead, she watched the failing lyse as the chanting continued, soothing and restful. Gradually the lines of pain lessened and the lyse's hands stopped their aimless plucking and lay quiet atop the blanket. His breathing slowed and deepened.

Runa passed a gentle hand over the old lyse's head, glancing over at Linn as she did so. "Now you see my gift at work. They call it a healing gift, but right now . . ." She shook her head and her plaits flopped against her back. "No. I do not heal these. They are beyond healing. The best I can do is help them live awhile longer, until the hope from the west appears to release them."

Linn fought to keep the tears that welled up in her eyes from spilling over. "Th-thank you, Runa," she faltered. "Thank you, Eavan. Excuse me." And she turned and fled into the forest, away from the disappointment in Runa's eyes, the sadness in Eavan's, and the smell of Berke's impending death.

She stumbled away, blinded by tears that she could no longer hold back. Then she fell to her knees at the foot of a giant tree and wept until her tears turned to dry sobs of despair. They tasted bitter in the back of her throat, underscoring the bitterness in her heart. "I can't do it. I cannot do it, Great One." She bent forward and muttered the words into her tunic. "Please don't make me go. I can't bear it!"

Bit by bit, her sobs lessened until they became periodic hiccups. She wiped her nose on her sleeve and rocked back on her bent legs to lean against the tree. She closed her eyes, calm with despair and a sense of doom.

And then the lysetett began to pulse, gently, steadily. A tiny breeze, no more than a breath, brushed her face. It smelled salty and cold, reminding her of the little beach the kjaerdyrer had brought her to. Then, steady and sure, the path she'd followed unfolded once more, this time in her mind's eye. Every blade of grass, every variation of color stood out crisply. Now, instead of bending to the east, the path ran arrow-straight due north.

Linn's eyes flew open. Thom stood before her, grave and quiet. His face was weary, but his eyes were sharp with knowing. "You've made your decision, then?" he asked.

"Yes." She drew in a long, quavering breath. "I accept the test. I will look for Maer's Lake."

Sixteen

Tap. Tap tap.

Linn opened the door of Thom's room. The lantern he carried shone on his glassy eyes, the lids puffy and red. Linn wondered if he'd gotten any sleep at all on his makeshift bed in the common room.

Her worry turned to alarm as the pair shared a scratched-together mornmeal and loaded the last of the gear in Linn's pack. They'd spent the previous evening in his room, avoiding the other lysefolk and using as few words as possible to decide what Linn should take on her journey. The reaction of the other lysefolk had been partly responsible for this painful silence. Linn had announced her decision from the dais. The lysefolk had slipped silently away, bowing to Linn as they passed out of the tower room, leaving her alone with Thom. Now Thom staggered through the packing, barely saying a word.

Finally he took her outside to where Maren and Liam awaited them in the cold early morning sunlight. Thom looked briefly into Linn's eyes. "The Great One will be with you, Linn." Then he disappeared back inside. Linn swallowed the aching lump that rose in her throat. She'd never felt so alone before, not even after the worst of Domm's beatings.

Maren's face was unreadable. "Come, Linnet," she said, waiting while Linn hoisted the pack onto her back and picked up Faerin. They made their way to the white beach, where Cam waited patiently in the skiff. Without a word, Linn waded to the smallboat and climbed inside. Then Maren raised her hand in farewell. "May the Great One guide you and bring you safely back to us."

Swish. Plonk. Swish. Plonk. Only Cam's even strokes broke the silence, first along the north shore of the island and then through the warm mist farther out. Linn huddled in the skiff, watching Faerin glide happily through the water.

"Chirrup?" His head broke the bay's surface, his flat ears dripping little beads of water. He clambered aboard the skiff with one powerful thrust, rocking the port side down so far that Linn thought the smallboat would capsize.

"Amazing creatures. Aren't they?" Cam spoke in short phrases to accommodate his strokes. "Brave as lions. Fierce as eagles. Never seen one. Quite so gentle. Always like that?"

Linn nodded. "Yes. He's been very friendly, right from the first. I guess he likes me." She tickled the kjaerdyr's ear. Faerin blinked.

"No telling. What Great One's. Creatures will do. Keep an eye. On this one. He's devoted. Never leave you."

Cam shipped his oars, and the skiff bumped into a spit of sand. "Well! Here we are."

Linn stared at Cam. "Already?" She looked up at the sun. "Midmorn so soon?" She glanced at the shoreline. "What should I do, Cam?"

The lyse squinted at the beach. "Well, I'd start by getting out of the skiff. If you're really the Hidden Arrow, the Great One will guide you. If not, I'd head for Sand." He pointed southwest.

There was nothing left to say. She eased herself onto the sand spit, and Cam heaved her pack out of the skiff. Faerin slid into the water and waddled up onto the narrow strip of beach.

Cam pushed off with one oar. "Don't worry, Linn!" he shouted. "Liam believes you're the Arrow, and he's rarely wrong about anything!"

Linn watched the skiff glide out of sight. Faerin wrapped himself around her calves. "*Chirrup?*" he inquired again.

"Who knows?" she replied. "I guess we just wait."

She stood on the shore for a long time, willing the path-finding gift to spring into action. Nothing happened. She closed her eyes, gritted her teeth, prayed with all her might. Still nothing. Finally, feeling desperate, she loaded the pack on her back, perched Faerin atop it, and just walked due north, as the previous day's vision had shown her.

The land north of Trebay was a tangle of twisted old trees and root-bound earth that made for rough going. Ancient stumps thrust their way through years of dead leaves. Smaller cousins to the huge boulders that lined the Farness tripped Linn up from their hiding places beneath the fallen foliage.

But the worst thing about hiking through this forest was the silence. No bird sang from its trees. No hares scuttled among its leaves. Linn strained to hear stealthy footsteps, the crack of a twig, anything. She stopped frequently to look behind her, but a sense of urgency pushed her to walk as fast as she could.

Over and over, the dark figure in the woods invaded her thoughts. Could it still be following her? And what about that shadow by the Farness? Did the tree trunks around her hide its silver form? Twice, between gnarled branches, she glimpsed a falcon gliding overhead. Even this seemed ominous in the cold depths of the wood.

"We haven't gone very far, have we?" she asked Faerin. The sun hung low in the sky. "We might as well stop here. It will be dark soon, and we can't stumble around this forest at night."

Thom had shown her how to pack sparely but well.

The outer pockets of the pack held small necessities: salt, flints, dried herbs, tea, a cake of hard soap, a face flannel. A full leather waterskin hung from the pack's bottom, along with a compact bedroll, two metal pans, a miniature shovel, and a hatchet. Inside the pack she discovered a wicked-looking knife, a metal cup and plate, a small wheel of cheese, a flask of mead, flatbread, strips of dried meat, dried fruit, and dren, small fish packed in oil inside a corked bottle. "At least we won't starve."

Linn gathered dry twigs and hacked up brittle lengths of fallen branches to start a fire. She cleared a space in the dirt, scavenging flat rocks to use as a fire ring. Once Faerin saw what she was up to, he joined in, using his strong tail to sweep away debris. Linn built the fire, lit it with her flints, and heated water for tea. She threw a couple of dren to Faerin.

"*Chirrr,*" he rumbled, licking his whiskers clean of the oil the dren were packed in. He waddled over to the fire and sniffed the air. "*Mmr, mmr.*" He begged for more.

"No, glutton," she said with a laugh. "These are mine." A thin stream of smoke rose from the pan where Linn's fish sizzled. She took a deep sniff and licked her lips with anticipation. She loved dren. They were smoky and dark and firm.

She drank her tea and offered Faerin water in her cupped hands. He shuffled over to the bedroll and curled up. Linn banked the fire and joined him. Despite her full stomach, she lay awake for a long time, tense and alert for any sound in the quiet that surrounded her. But eventually Faerin's warmth and her own tiredness overcame her fear and she slept.

Plunk.

Linn's eyes flew open. The fire had sunk to ruddy embers. Faerin stirring in his own sound slumber must have awakened her, or maybe a small animal in the underbrush. Linn wormed deeper into the bedroll and gazed dreamily into the remains of her fire, sure that sleep would return quickly.

"Linnet." The sound, barely a whisper, cut through the darkness surrounding her. There was no mistaking it. Someone had spoken her name.

Her nerves stretched taut, alert for any tiny movement, while her heart hammered in her chest. She lifted her head cautiously from the ground.

"Hello?" Despite Linn's fear, her voice sounded steady and low.

No response. But her ears picked up a light noise. A sigh.

It came from across the fire. Moving almost as quietly as Thom could, she eased up onto her hands and knees to stare into the blackness. A quick movement flickered in the thick shadows across the fire. Then, as her eyes became more accustomed to the darkness, she saw who sat beside her fire out here in the middle of nowhere.

It was Mam.

Linn clutched the bedroll, accidentally dumping Faerin out into the cold. He sat on his haunches and sniffed the breeze with an air of puzzlement. *"Chirrup?"* he questioned, moving closer to Linn.

"Mam, is it really you?" Linn's voice quavered. "How did you know where I was? And what about the sted? Did you leave the babies alone with Domm?" She got to her feet and looked about wildly, half expecting to see Peri and Fen toddling toward her out of the night.

Her mother's face stretched into an unaccustomed smile, and she shook her head. "Yes, it's me. And no, I didn't leave the children alone with Domm—he's got far too much to do. They're staying at Ilar's sted over the hill. His mother is caring for them nicely, and you know how Ilar loves children."

Linn nodded mutely, still in shock. Mam was here, before her, in this lonely place. She'd cared enough to come after Linn, cared enough to track her down and find her. Warmth crept into Linn's heart, replacing her numbness with a soaring feeling of hope. *Mam loves me—she's here to share my trial and protect me!* Linn's eyes filled with tears. "You'll stay with me? I must complete this journey—it's rather complicated but I think I may be a lyse, and . . ." She trailed off. Better to explain later. "You'll come with me on my trip?"

Mam coughed, clutching a rough goat-hair shawl around her neck. Her face, normally the color of a well-done biscuit, shone pale in the darkness surrounding her. "No," she replied slowly, "I can't come with you. In fact, I'm here to bring you home. I couldn't let you go as things were. I spoke to Domm after you left, and we worked out another arrangement."

"Another arrangement?" Linn's eyes widened. "What do you mean?"

"Come back to Laefe with me now. We won't force you to marry Tykk or anyone else against your will." Mam smiled again, and her hands fluttered against her throat.

Linn stared. Backing away from the betrothal he'd arranged didn't sound like her stepfather at all. "I don't understand. Domm beat me when I said no to the betrothal. He was willing to force me then. Why would he change his mind?"

"He wants you back on Laefe. He truly does." Mam's eyes shifted back and forth, avoiding Linn's gaze. "He gave me his solemn word that he would not force you now."

"But why does he want me back? And what has his word been worth in the past? The only one he's ever kept was to not make you become Ranite."

That seemed to upset Mam. She wrung her hands and shifted her weight uneasily. "Now, now, daughter," she said. "Domm is an honorable man. He's willing to compromise. Let's discuss the proposal he offers you."

Linn squinted through the shadows, trying to gauge

her mother's true feelings. Surely she didn't really believe all that muck about Domm being an honorable man. And as for compromise . . . Domm didn't know the meaning of the word. For one thing, he didn't trust anyone else, not even his wife, to keep an agreement. And he would never allow her to offer a compromise on his behalf.

"Why would Domm send you to bring me back?" Linn's question was directed more at herself than at Mam. Sweat broke out on her forehead as her initial confusion turned to fear. She returned to her first question. "How did you find me?"

Mam blinked. "What's happened to you, Linn? You're so suspicious! Who's turned you against your own family?"

Linn gave a bleak laugh. "Ha! As if I were ever a part of Domm's family!"

Mam's hands started to flutter about her throat again. "You just don't understand Domm, Linnet. He's not a bad man. He wants to do what's best for the family and you. I know he's not your father. But Domm loves you as best he can. And he feels terrible about driving you away from Laefe. Come home with me now, my girl. Things will be different. You'll see."

Linn began to shake. "Stop lying! All this talk about him loving me is nonsense! Now answer my question, Mam! How did you find me?"

Mam stirred, rising now to crouch closer to the fire,

her face lit by the fire's embers. A round red tattoo glinted from Mam's forehead, the mate to Domm's own. "How did I find you? I was sent by my master, daughter."

"Mam." Linn's lower lip quivered. "What did he do to you?" Her legs wobbled, and she stumbled and fell to her knees.

Mam touched the red circle. "I came to my senses, daughter. Why fight any longer? It's so much easier to submit. You'll find that out—easier than fighting."

Mam's eyes locked on Linn's, willing her to obey. Linn tore her gaze away. "No, no!" Linn whimpered. "You didn't let him do that to you! You didn't submit to Rane—you couldn't!"

"I did, daughter." Mam crooned the words. "And soon you will, too. You will be at peace. No more struggle, no more pain or fear. Just peace." Her voice was mesmerizing. "Come to me. Come with me. Find peace." Mam began moving toward Linn. She lifted one bare foot above the fire.

"Watch out!" Linn managed to choke out just as her mother's foot landed squarely in the heart of the burning embers. "The fire—"

Too late. Horrified, Linn looked into Mam's face, expecting to see it distorted with agony. But her expression hadn't changed. She still stared at Linn, intent and beguiling.

Linn's skin puckered, and the hair on the back of her

neck stood erect. "No. No." She backed away until her shoulders came up against the rough bark of a tree.

"*Hiissss!*" Faerin moved between the pair. His back was arched, his claws extended their full length. His teeth gleamed in the firelight. "*Sssss.*"

Mam hesitated. Her body began to shake with a barely discernible tremor.

"*Rrrrr.*" Faerin growled, shook his head, and advanced a step.

"Call off your beast, daughter. I mean you no harm!"

Linn shook her head. "No!"

"Now, Linnet, you know your own mother. Would I ever hurt you? Would I ever desert you? What kind of mother would do that to her own child?"

A tear rolled down Linn's cheek. She'd known nothing but desertion from Mam. All Domm's beatings, all the humiliation he'd heaped on her head . . . No matter how much she longed to believe it, Linn knew that Mam was weak and empty inside. Beaten in every way but one.

Mam had drawn a single line in the quicksand of her life. She had never submitted to Rane. She had held Domm to the agreement he'd made at their betrothal. She'd given way in every other area to ensure that he kept that one agreement. Was it because being a Truen was the only bit of Farr she'd managed to hang on to? Mam was weak—she'd abandoned Linn to Domm— but she had not, would not become a Ranite.

"What kind of mother would do that?" Linn countered. She raised a trembling finger and pointed at the figure. "A human mother—my mother! Something you are not and never could be!"

The figure began to shake in earnest. Faerin moved protectively to Linn's side as the form softened and blurred. The colors of skin and clothing melted into one another, and a wail emerged from the dissolving mouth. With a final cry, the figure disappeared into the night. A faint stench hung in the air. It smelled of Rane—the Rane Linn had confronted aboard the *Dark Dragon*.

Staggering a little, Linn picked up the kjaerdyr, stroking his fur so that it lay sleek and smooth once more. She clutched Faerin to her chest and wrapped the bedroll around them both. She crouched there shivering and rocking until the morning light feathered the sky. Then she slept.

Seventeen

"Which way should I go? What should I do?"
Linn balanced atop a large boulder in the
woods. A shaft of light warmed her face and hands. The
small section of sky she could see through the tree
canopy was pale and cloudy.

"Please, Great One, please! Open the way—make the
gift work today! Please!" Desperation made her voice
higher than normal.

Trembling, she jumped off the rock to stand next to
a sapling. She closed her eyes. "Please, oh, please!" she
breathed. She opened her eyes and reached out to touch
the sapling.

Nothing. It didn't move, it didn't shake, it didn't bow.
Nothing.

She collapsed to the ground. Faerin tickled her face
with his whiskers, and she hugged his neck.

"What should we do? What *can* we do?"

Faerin waddled over to the pack and pushed it with his nose. *"Chirr!"*

"All right." She sighed and got to her feet, heaving the pack up onto her back. Faerin swarmed up her arm and curled around her neck. "I guess we have no choice. We just have to go north, as the vision showed me. And hope that it was sent by the Great One."

Linn trudged on and on, casting anxious looks around her and occasionally testing her direction by checking for moss on tree trunks. It always grew on a tree's north side. When midday came, she decided to keep walking. "Sorry, Faerin, but we're going to skip midmeal."

"Rowr!" He jumped off her pack and blocked her way.

"No! I don't want to stop. Let's just keep going— maybe we can still make it out of the woods before night." She looked nervously over her shoulder. "I don't want another meeting like last night's!"

"Ro-owr!" He took her wounded hand in his mouth and shook it gently.

"All right," she conceded. "We'll stop. But only to eat something cold." She tossed the last two dren to Faerin and chewed on a slab of dried meat and drank some water before hoisting the pack and Faerin on her back again.

Linn had walked a couple of hours when she suddenly stopped short and gasped. Instead of a gradual thinning of the woods, instead of grassy fields dotted with occasional autumn-bare trees and low-growing bushes, the forest ended abruptly. Before her, a huge, bare moor rolled out to the horizon, its gray-green surface marked with gigantic mossy wrinkles.

Faerin jumped down and rolled over on his back, his face blissful. Linn kneeled and ran her hands over the ground cover at her feet. "Nice. Springy and soft." The plants felt cool and soothing against her wound. "Aaah," she sighed. Then she put her hand to her ribs as the lysetett began to pulse, gently but insistently.

At her feet, the tiny leaves of the ground cover shrank and pressed together. Already close to the earth, they couldn't bend any lower. "The gift! Faerin, the gift, it's working!" The path was a mere shadow, a slightly different color than the surrounding plants. But it was the path.

Her fear last night, the Ranite tattoo on Mam's forehead, her melting face—Linn pushed it all to the back of her mind. She flung her arms straight in the air. "Thank you! Thank you, Great One!" She kissed her wound and raised her hand again. "Thanks to you—the True God!"

"*Chirr. Chi-ir.*" Faerin pushed his head against her knee.

Relief poured out of Linn in a joyful laugh. "All right, all right. We'll get going." She shaded her eyes and took a long look around. "No trees, Faerin. We don't want to freeze, do we? We'll have to bring some firewood with us."

She dumped her pack on the ground, pulled out her hatchet, and walked back into the woods, whistling. Sticks were easy to find, but she'd have to cut small logs. It took about an hour before she was satisfied with the pile of wood. She strapped it into a faggot with her belt and a bit of rope. "There," she said, giving the faggot a good shake. "That should do. I'll just drag it along."

She adjusted the pack, straightened her shoulders, and glanced back at Faerin, lying flat on the faggot bundle. Then she peered down at the ground cover, ready for the gift to show her the way.

The gift was working—the quivering lysetett told her that—but she couldn't see the path. Linn closed her eyes, breathing deeply and slowly. "Great One, help me, please! It's here, I know! Give me eyes to see it!"

The lysetett reacted again. This time the threads didn't pull but drove deep into Linn. A vision of roots sinking into her chest, her heart, her bowels, appeared in her mind. She stilled her fear, calmed her tense body, and reached down inside herself, plunging to the place the lysetett touched.

"Ooooh." Now she could see it. A door opened inside her, connecting her eyes with some other sense she didn't know she had. A place touched by whatever it was that touched the plants, bending them into a path.

Linn rose to her feet and took several steps forward.

The lysetett sprang to attention. Suddenly a protected patch of moss on the underside of a rock pointed the way, delicate and light. Another step. And another. A sheltered inch or so of ground cover, deep inside a wrinkle in the moor, bent and twisted to show her which way to go.

Following this path was slow work. Linn had to be doubly alert, sensitive to any tiny change in color, density, and shading of the mossy cover. The moor's deep wrinkles made the path even more difficult to find. By nightfall her body ached with fatigue, and her overworked mind could no longer make the effort to concentrate. After a small fire and a quick bite to eat, she wrapped the bedroll around her, snuggled next to Faerin, and fell instantly asleep. But it was not a peaceful rest. Nightmares crowded into her slumbers, horrible, helpless ones that made her twitch and moan but would not release her to consciousness.

"Nooooooo!" She shot straight up, her breathing shallow and eyes staring. *Just a dream. Just a dream.* Linn closed her eyes and made herself breathe more deeply. "It's all right. 'S all right." She stroked Faerin when he laid his head on her leg.

Mam! The dream had been of Mam, trapped on the deck of the *Dark Dragon*, Rane looming over her. He'd bent down closer and closer until Mam had opened her mouth and—

Linn shuddered. The sky was just beginning to light

up on the horizon. "Come on, Faerin, we might as well get going."

The sun rose, but it didn't bring much warmth. Faerin's breath formed a white cloud about his head, and the moor sparkled with white frost. Linn warmed her hands at the fire, threw on just one more log, and shared a hurried mornmeal with Faerin. But when it came time to start off, the path did not appear.

"What's wrong?" Linn knelt on the moss, searching for any sign of movement. "Why doesn't the gift work?" She ran her wounded hand over the ground, melting the frost that covered it.

Immediately the plants responded, twisting to point the way. "Thank the Great One! But how are we going to follow the path now? I can't crawl all the way to Maer's Lake!"

"*Rar!*" Faerin's short bark drew Linn to his side. His nose was buried in a deep wrinkle in the moorland, one that had protected the plants within it from the frost. Linn touched them, and immediately they bent in the same direction as the others.

Looking for clear ground made the first few hours of the day drag. Linn moved so slowly that Faerin abandoned the faggot and waddled about, inspecting the ground and trailing Linn. When the sun rose enough to melt the frost, he resumed his post atop the bundle of wood, and Linn made better time.

But at nightfall she wasn't tired enough to shake off

her worries. She tossed and twitched in her bedroll, afraid to fall asleep in case she had another dream about Mam and Rane. Finally she sank into a restless doze.

When she awoke, the early morning lay just at the horizon's edge. A faint and cold gray light bled up into the sky. All of Linn's senses were alert, on guard against *something*. No sound, no movement, no scents. But something was out there, she was sure of it. Faerin's back tensed against hers, his hackles stiff. She could feel the vibration of a soundless growl in his chest. Something, or someone, lay in wait nearby.

Linn peered over the top of her blanket. The gray light drained the landscape of color. The ground, the faggot, even her pack were covered with rime. Atop the pack, glinting in the faint light, lay her knife.

She worked her hand out of her bedroll, then humped along the ground to her pack. Her arm stretched for the knife, her fingers closing around the handle. She pulled it toward her. Now she had a weapon just in case—

Thud! A large, smelly boot pinned Linn's wrist to the ground, and a soft, gloating chuckle invaded the silence. Linn twisted around to stare up at her aggressor.

Domm!

Her stepfather loomed above her, his red tattoo blazing in the gray light of dawn. He pressed his boot harder against Linn's wrist, twisting it painfully until she had to release the knife. With a grunt he bent down and picked it up. He backed away a few steps, handling the knife lightly as if it were a child's toy instead of a sharp iron blade.

"Where did you come from?" Her voice was barely a whisper.

"So you didn't believe your mother?" he asked, ignoring her question.

Linn began to sweat. Her wounded hand throbbed and ached as it had the day Domm scarred her. "That wasn't my mother," she whispered, her voice scratchy and strange.

He picked up a twig and began to peel the bark delicately from it, tiny strip by tiny strip. Again he ignored her words. "So you think to prove yourself a lyse, eh? As I told you back on Laefe, I have other plans for you. And they don't include any lysefolk." He pointed the tip of the blade at Linn's face. "Tykk is waiting for you, although no doubt he's growing more impatient every day."

Linn touched the place under her tunic where the Lysetome lay hidden. A brief burst of strength shot through her. "I don't belong to you or Tykk *or* Rane! And I won't go back with you—I'd rather die first!"

"That, my girl, can be arranged," Domm said, advancing toward her.

Linn scrambled from the bedroll, kicking it from her legs. Fear and loathing made her clumsy. *Get away get away get away!* The shriek tore through her mind, and her wounded hand pounded with pain.

"*Ssss!*" Faerin rose from the bedroll, hissing through his strong white teeth. His thick fur stood on end, and his eyes were wild with aggression as he advanced to stand in front of Linn. "*Hiissss!*"

Domm stopped abruptly in his tracks. "Do you think a baby animal can protect you from *me*?" he asked, his voice thick with derision. But in the growing light from the rising sun, Linn saw the knife shaking in his grasp.

That trembling knife made her take a closer look at Domm. In the daylight his skin looked gray and loose, as if it didn't fit his bones. His eyes had the glassy cast of a drunkard about to pass out from too much ale. But his tattoo had a malicious life of its own. It glared at Linn from the center of his forehead.

He's not Domm. The realization did not comfort her. If the Mam beside her fire had been a creature of Rane, then this thing must be too. On shaking legs Linn struggled to her feet, fear pumping through her body. But before that fear turned to horror, the lysetett began to pulse. Strength ran through her, squeezing out fear. Her legs stopped shaking, and Linn lifted her chin to address the creature before her.

"He's not just any animal. He belongs to the Great One and you know it, don't you?" Faerin hissed again, advancing a step or two toward the figure. Its thick fingers tightened their grasp on the handle, and the knife in its hand stopped shaking. Without a word, it brought the blade high in the air, ready to plunge it into Faerin's body.

Before Linn could release the scream that rose in her throat, something else screamed high above them. An eagle, giving full voice, hurtled down toward the group. Surely it would crash into the ground! But it didn't. At the very last second, the bird spread its wings and leveled out. Its extended talons sank into the nape fur of the kjaerdyr's neck. The eagle rose into the air and turned south, its catch hanging limply in its grasp.

"Faerin!" Linn's throat closed, thick with unshed tears. She turned back to the Domm creature, too choked up to speak.

The figure twirled the blade's handle between its hands, a cruel smile lighting its eyes. "Well, daughter, it's just you and me now." It stepped toward her, grasping the knife's handle again and holding it as though it had no hesitation about using it. The creature bent down and cut away one of the pack's leather straps. "Let's see if a good beating will teach you not to defy me."

Linn flinched as the strap flicked against Domm's leggings, but she didn't give ground. Her stepfather's figure took another step toward her, breathing heavily through its mouth. The stench of its breath hit Linn full in the face. Raw and sweet and decayed . . .

"You're not Domm," she whispered. "You're not human. So just what *are* you? Rane?"

The figure advanced another step, a smile plastered across its gray face. "Don't you know? We've met twice before."

Another rush of stench almost overpowered Linn. She retreated a step, coughing. "How did you find me? And why have you been hunting me all this time?"

"Think, my dear." His voice made the endearment obscene. "I'm always looking for new converts. And you would be most welcome, believe me."

Linn shuddered, wrapping her arms protectively around her torso. Once again she felt the Lysetome under her tunic. This time she pulled it out and held it before her.

"I am a Truen. I'll never be yours!" Linn stepped forward and extended her wounded hand, palm up. "Faerin wasn't just any animal, and I'm not just any girl." She took another step. "And here's the proof. Here's the mark of the Hidden Arrow on my palm, where my stepfather hurt me. I belong to the Great One, and I call on him now to protect me!"

The gray face sagged, as though whatever had animated it had fled. The Ranite tattoo on its forehead began to smolder, hotter and hotter, until it burned blue. Flames sprang from it, licking greedily at now-colorless skin. The smell of burning flesh rose on the morning wind, making Linn gasp. Domm's face formed one last derisive smile before it became unrecognizable. She closed her eyes and turned away. When she looked again, the figure had gone. All that remained was a whiff of the sweet, cloying scent Linn had first smelled that night on the *Dark Dragon*. Death.

Eighteen

lack. Clack. The stones made a hard, echoing noise in the quiet of the moor. One more would do. There. Now Faerin's cairn was complete. It had taken nearly half a day, but grief had driven Linn to search out enough stones to finish the task. He was gone, and tears were not enough to express her sorrow. But the cairn was a lasting memorial to him.

She returned to her campsite and numbly mended the leather strap the creature had torn off her pack. She hoisted it onto her back, hesitating over the faggot. What was the use? She left the wood behind and went on.

Grief made the gift dull inside her, slowing her progress. But she pushed herself to continue walking, searching out the path until the last rays of the sun faded away. She ate only enough to still her stomach's rumbling. That night she slept little. And the next day her steps grew heavier, her mind wearier.

She almost missed the change in the distant land-scape, she'd become so fixed on the path at her feet. But the land began to rise steadily, huge boulders jutting from their mossy cover as if shrugging off a blanket. It forced her to look ahead.

Along the horizon swelled the foothills of some far-off mountain range. They were dotted with stands of evergreens and clumps of bare white birches. Now the path was easier to follow. Grasses replaced the ground cover of the moor. After three hours of climbing, Linn gained the top of a jagged hill and looked down on a huge lake. It lay deep in a valley among the foothills, a pointing black finger of liquid.

Maer's Lake? It didn't match the Lysetome's descrip-tion. What had happened to the golden water? But the sky was overcast, and the afternoon light waned. Maybe up close the water would be gold.

Her gift created a winding, zigzag path down the steep hillside. As she descended, the lysetett began to tug. Her chest grew warm, a spreading glow that ban-ished the cold from her body. Her heart lifted. She felt no sense of urgency, no rush to gain the lake's shore. Just a steady, humming happiness that seemed to say "home."

It was impossible to make the long hike to the lake before sunset. Because of the height of the hills sur-rounding her, the day ended sooner than Linn had ex-pected. Even though the lysetett continued to warm her, she gathered sticks and chopped a few logs to build a fire. She didn't bother to cook, though; she was too drained to eat. Instead she wrapped herself in her bedroll before the fire and slept through the night for the first time in days.

"Caw! Caw!" A huge black raven, perched in a nearby tree, awoke Linn early the next morning. Frost made her blanket stiff, and her nose was icy to the touch. She cut more wood for the fire and made herself some tea. After a few hard biscuits, she packed up and started down the hill again.

She didn't bother to try to find the path her gift might show her. The grasses all down the hill were white with rime, so the gift would not operate anyway. But that didn't matter. Her objective lay in sight: the lake in the valley below her, glistening as the sun's rays peeked over the hills to strike its dark surface.

It didn't take more than a couple of hours to reach the shore. Linn hesitated, despite the lysetett's tug. It hadn't been the overcast sky that had made the water look so dark the day before. It really *was* dark, a deep, black-brown color, as thick as the hot tar used by sailors to make their ships watertight. Its glossy skin reflected nothing. Could this really be Maer's Lake? She bent down to examine the tarry liquid that filled the lake bed.

"I've waited forever for this moment, Linnet."

She twirled around, heart hammering. A man hovered a few yards away in the shadow of a tree. Although it had been eleven seasons, Linn realized immediately who stood before her, apologetic and still.

It was Farr, alive and strong and well. Her own farr.

Linn stretched out her right hand, too stunned to speak. Farr stepped forward from the tree's shadow, a rueful smile on his face. He looked the same as Linn remembered, black hair and eyes, dark brown skin shiny from days in the sun and wind. Even his clothes—brown leather boots and belt, wool leggings, and a goat-hair tunic—seemed familiar to her.

"It's you!" She came closer, trying at the same time to hold her hope in check. "But I thought—we thought you were *dead*. You *were* dead, weren't you?"

Farr's smile widened, making a white slash in his dark face. "You know I was, Little Bird," he said.

"How in the Great One's name do you come to be here now, in the most deserted place in Maether?" Linn's lower lip trembled. Farr took a step toward her, and she held up her wounded hand. "Wait! How do I know you're really Farr? How do I know you're not Rane?"

"Would Rane remember our secrets? Would he know about the Lysetome I left you? Or the time you hid from me in the hold of my boat? Remember?" Now Farr held his hand out to her. "Remember? I promised I'd never leave you, never go from you. It was necessary to go for a while. But now I'm back to help you, to guide you." He took a step closer to Linn.

Tears began to run down her cheeks, and she crossed her arms over her chest, holding herself to stop the shaking in her body. "But you *did* leave me, Farr! You did leave me! Mam didn't help me—the Great One didn't help me! I was alone with Domm! He beat me and hated me and I was all alone!" Great sobs shook her body, and the tears pouring from her eyes almost blinded her.

"Shhh, shhh, my Little Bird. There now. It's all over. You'll never have to deal with Domm again. Never. I promise." Farr's hands patted the air before him, as though to soothe her.

"You don't understand, Farr," Linn replied, spittle clogging her throat. "I traveled to the City of Trees. They think I might be a lyse—I have a gift! A real one, just as you thought! It brought me here, to Maer's Lake, so I can take its water back to restore the skjolder and save the lysefolk. It's the only way to defeat Rane."

Farr's eyes widened. "They sent you to find it alone? *Alone?* How could anyone, never mind so young a girl, accomplish this task by herself? And you think this is Maer's Lake? Look around you." He pointed to the water. "Does that water look golden to you? Does it look sacred or pure? What you think is a gift has mis-led you. In fact, that's why the Great One sent me here.

To help you find the true Maer's Lake." He smiled kindly at her.

Hope surged inside her, but still Linn hesitated, trying to work things out logically. She herself had questioned whether this was Maer's Lake, hadn't she? The lake's brown-black water was the wrong color. Farr was right—this couldn't be Maer's Lake. And wouldn't it be better to follow Farr, to let him help her? Suddenly, finding the lake all by herself did seem impossible. Her entire trip to the City receded, becoming an unreal, fantastic dream.

The light strengthened as the sun rose higher in the sky. Immediately, the lysetett resumed its pulse. The threads stretched as fine as spun glass, sharp and pure and ready to sing like crystal with the right touch. Their insistence pulled her toward the black, tarry lake, wooing her irresistibly with their certainty. A gush of sheer joy pulsed through her body, and then she knew for sure. Linn turned back to Farr, ready to explain that this must be Maer's Lake.

He had crept up beside her and now stood close, yet not touching her. His brown skin was tinged with a touch of gray.

"Come, daughter, come with me now," he said quietly. "As I said, I've waited forever for this moment, to see my dear daughter again and hold her in my arms. Don't turn from me now that I've made the long journey back to you. Forget what Thom and the other lysefolk told you. Come away with me—we'll find the real Maer's Lake together."

More than anything in the world Linn longed to be folded in her father's embrace, for him to make everything all right. *I just want to be with my farr!* she wept inside, once more the four-season-old she had been. All her need, all her loneliness rushed up, blocking out the pull of the lysetett. She saw only her father standing before her, reaching out as she'd always dreamed. At last. At long last.

"Ca-ree! Ca-ree!" High above their heads, a hawk gave voice. The sound knifed through Linn's chest. She blinked and looked back into her father's eyes with more reason than emotion.

"Wait," she said, taking three abrupt steps back and holding up her wounded palm. "How do you know about Thom?"

Nineteen

Attic began in Farr's left eyelid. "Thom? Do I know a Thom?"

"You mentioned him just now. You said 'Thom and the other lysefolk' a minute ago."

Farr licked his lips. A sickly-sweet odor wafted to Linn, and her heart sank. How could she ever have taken this gray-tinged creature for her own farr? It was just a disguise, just another disguise for Rane. Linn backed away, glancing over her right shoulder. There was a long, thin spit of land that thrust out into the lake, and she edged toward it. The figure followed.

"But Linnet, I couldn't have said that; you must have misunderstood me. I know nothing about the lysefolk except the old stories."

Linn reached the spit and backed down it, hoping Rane hated the lake as Daern had said. The figure stopped. It stood there for a few moments, shaking. Finally it stepped reluctantly out onto the spit, dragging its feet through the sand. Her flesh crawled at the thought of this thing, this whatever-it-was, touching her, holding her. She gagged a little as the thing drew closer, closer, looking at her out of Farr's dark eyes, which were now as hard as flint.

"You are mine, girl," the figure said in a deep, sonorous voice. It sounded as if it came from a much larger chest than Farr's. "You're mine, and I'm here to take you. But I do offer you something in return."

"What do you mean? What do you have that I could possibly want?"

"Here. Look and you'll see." The creature cupped its right hand and twisted it in a figure eight in the air, then opened it slightly and muttered a word in another language. *"Bessire."* A flame appeared in its palm, so bright that it hurt Linn's eyes and she turned away. The figure smiled and gazed directly into the light. "Don't worry, girl. It won't blind you. Look."

She turned back and focused on the silvery light. At first it flickered in the wind from the lake, but then it settled and burned steadily. "I don't see anything. Just the fla—oh!" A scene appeared in the flame, tiny but so real that Linn drew closer. Then she heard the figures in the scene talking to each other.

Gee and Tarkin, on board the *Dark Dragon.* The boy's

face was radiant, blazing with joy as he gazed up at his father. Tarkin's head bent down over Gee's, and his arm encircled him.

"Fa, are we really going back to Baln? Are we really going back home to Mam and Mia?" Tears glistened in the corners of Gee's eyes.

Tarkin nodded, then squinted up into the sun, shading his eyes with one hand. "We'll be there within the week. And I'm going to take an entire season off just so we can make up for lost time. Just the four of us together again." He turned back to Gee, and as his hand dropped to his side, Linn had a clear view of his forehead. No Ranite tattoo scarred its surface. It was clear and smooth, free of worry and care. Tarkin's eyes were limpid, filled only with love for Gee.

The scene faded. Linn covered her mouth with her wounded hand and looked up at the creature. "You would do this for Gee—for me? You would release Tarkin from his slavery to you?"

The Farr-thing nodded. "But that's not all I offer. Look."

Linn gazed into the flame again. This time Domm's sted appeared. Jenna, Peri, and Bran pranced around their mother, hugging her legs with their slender little arms. Carey held Fen on his shoulders. Then Carey gave the baby to Mam, and turned with a laugh to chase the other three around the plank table. But it was Mam who held Linn's eye. She was a different person. Her shoulders and back were straight, her hair shone with life, and all the wrinkles and bruises on her face had been smoothed away.

"Carey!" Mam's voice was light and cheerful. "Now, Carey, stop encouraging them!" She laughed then—Mam actually laughed! "Come on now, help me get evenmeal on the table before Fa gets back." The children scurried around, placing bread and cheese and meat on the table.

"Where's my family?" A big voice boomed at the door.

"Fa! Fa!" The little ones scrambled to be the first to greet the man who stood there. He entered the room and opened his arms in welcome. Linn peered at the man's face. It wasn't Domm—it was Ilar, the man who lived across the valley from the sted. Never married, Ilar was known all over Laefe for his cheerful good humor and way with children. He had no tattoo on his forehead.

"See?" Rane's voice whispered in Linn's ear. "See. I could make this happen for your mother and brothers and sister. They could be happy the rest of their lives, if you will just . . . *cooperate*."

The scene vanished from the flame, but Linn continued to stare. "Happy?" she murmured. "They could be happy forever? Free from Domm and the Ranites? And I can make this happen? But how? What—"

"I have more to show you. I realize that I"—it

brushed a hand down its front—"am not the farr you once knew. But that can be remedied quite easily . . ." The flame flickered again, then burned more brightly and fiercely than before. And this time, Linn felt herself drawn into the scene that appeared.

She stood on the beach at the City of Trees, hand in hand with Farr. The *real* Farr. His face glowed in the soft light of morning, healthy and strong and true. No tattoo marred his forehead, no scent of death passed his lips. His arm lay as heavy and warm as Faerin around Linn's shoulders as he looked down at her. Approval lit his face, and his eyes were soft and gentle. "My daughter, my Little Bird. You brought me back—you brought me home! Home to be with you!"

The Linn in the scene sighed with contentment, and the real Linn echoed that sigh. Complete happiness filled her heart, and a tear slid down her cheek. "I can be with my real farr? I can live in the City with him— for always?"

Again the being that was not Farr nodded.

"But how can this happen?"

The creature laughed, a gloating little moan. "I am the Master. I am Rane. And the whole world lives—or dies—in my hand." It flourished its flame. "All you have to do to make these things happen is just obey me."

The scenes in the flame danced in Linn's head, and their happiness and joy filled her heart. *I could make Gee happy, Mam happy, and the children and Carey! And I could be with Farr, in the City of Trees forever—forever!* It took her breath away, just the thought, just the possibility of it. She hugged herself with glee, clutching the hidden Lysetome to her heart.

The warmth of the lysetett became a scorching blaze. *All that is good, all that is holy, all that is pure dwells in the Great One's hand.* The quote from the Lysetome rang in her head. *Good—clang! Holy—clang! Pure—clang! His—clang!* And then Linn remembered another quote, one she'd memorized long ago when Domm had first started to beat her. *Who is good but the Great One alone?* She shook her head, then looked at the creature with clear eyes.

"Who *is* good but the Great One?" she breathed. The gray being before her closed its eyes. "Who made the world for his pleasure, who will never desert me, in the water or in the flame? Who holds the world in his palm?" Linn spat on the ground. "Not you—not Rane!"

The figure shimmered and shook. A black mist poured from its mouth, winding around its head and body, encasing it in darkness. When the mist cleared, Farr's figure was gone, and in its place stood the beautiful silver giant Linn had seen on the deck of the *Dark Dragon*, the flame still burning in its right palm.

"Oh!" Linn had forgotten how breathtakingly beautiful Rane could be.

It lifted its perfect lip and sneered down on her. "So, you are having second thoughts about my bargain? Are you sure? Think carefully and choose wisely, girl. And here, to make your decision a little easier—" It bent down to the lake, flexed its hand wide open, and touched the black surface with the silver flame.

Fwoosh! Immediately the thick black liquid ignited. The fire spread over the entire expanse of the lake until the whole thing roared to the sky, a silver inferno surrounding Linn.

Rane straightened up and took a step toward her. "It's your choice. Life and happiness for those you love." It gestured toward the lake. "Or choose the flames. Either way, your life as the Hidden Arrow is over."

Linn backed as far down the spit of land as she could, her heels almost touching the flames. They snapped and hissed all around her, licking her with heat. Nowhere to go. Nothing she could do would save her now. With trembling hands she drew out the Lysetome. It fell open, and she read aloud what was written there. "Choose life, even if it ends in death."

She looked up into Rane's hard silver face. Its beauty took her breath away still, yes. But she no longer felt tempted by the things she'd seen in its hand. Mam had made her choice, as Gee had his. Now she would make hers.

She jumped.

As she'd jumped from the deck of the *Dark Dragon* into the unknown sea, so she jumped now. Without thought, without hope, without a plan. Down she went, past the fire into the inky, tarry depths of the thick liquid that filled Maer's Lake. It parted to make way for her, closing over her head with a hiss of flame.

Linn fell through the substance slowly. She held her breath as she sank through the dark ooze around her. It clung to her body, coating her ears, her nose, her eyes, her mouth. She fell and fell and fell until she thought she must be close to the lake's bottom. But still, she continued falling.

Her lungs burned, warning her that they must have the air they craved or they would suck in the thick liquid surrounding her. Her chest shuddered with the effort of holding her breath, and desperate tears squeezed past her lids to encounter tarry blackness.

Then, suddenly and past any reason, someone took her hand.

Twenty

The hand was strong and huge, engulfing her child-sized one in its own weighty mass. As comforting as a parent's hand holding that of a son or daughter, the grasp warmed her with a careless intimacy born out of certain knowledge and acceptance.

"Linnet." Somehow the sound of her name traveled through the thick liquid that coated her ears. It wasn't her mother, it wasn't Domm, it wasn't Thom or Maren or even Farr. It wasn't breathy or earthshaking or frightening. It was familiar, it was intimate, it was *loved*. The sound of it reached down into Linn's chest and ran over the lysetett, making the spun-glass threads vibrate like crystal. "Breathe."

Breathe? Linn's eyes popped open. Instead of the black inkiness she expected, she saw a figure. Huge and vital and golden, carefully holding her hand in his own. She couldn't make out his face or body, but he was there, a

golden being that vibrated with acceptance and knowledge and goodness.

For a fleeting moment, Linn caught a glimpse of his
face. He opened his mouth to speak, and a caressing
breath that smelled of lavender and cedar and ripe,
sweet fruit rolled toward her. "Breathe, Linnet," he said
again. His face glowed, as though lit by a friendly fire in
a cozy winter room. And his eyes—not hard black flint
or flat blue disks, but deep and laughing and eager, urg-
ing her on, taking pleasure in her efforts. "Breathe," he
repeated, laughing.

So she did. She closed her eyes, opened her mouth,
and breathed in the thick black liquid in which she sank
until it filled her nasal passages, her throat, her lungs.
And still she kept breathing, deeper and deeper and
more and more, until she thought her whole body must
be full of the tarry liquid and she would sink to the
bottom of the lake to die.

But instead, it buoyed her. She rose, a bubble in a
boiling pot, to the surface of the lake, holding tightly to
the massive hand of the Great One.

She broke through the water's surface suddenly,
coughing and sputtering. She paddled inexpertly over to
the shore, dragging her body up to collapse on the sand.

"*Chirrup.*"

"Faerin!" His face appeared next to her head.
He nuzzled her neck and arms and legs as if to make
sure she was really there. Linn put her left arm around

him and pulled the kjaerdyr close, tears pouring down her face.

"I've never seen a more bedraggled pair than the two of you," said a voice directly over Linn's head. She looked up, too weary to be on her guard anymore. The bare branches of a tree overhung the lake, and she could easily see the figure perched above her. Her face relaxed into a smile, a smile that stretched her cheeks as far as they would go and made their muscles ache.

"Thom." The name brought the lyse down from the branch to crouch at her head. Thom grinned as he took her right hand, covering it up with his gloved ones. She hiccuped, then let loose a giggle. "You always catch me looking my best."

The lyse threw back his head and laughed, and when he looked down again Linn saw one tear fall from his eye. She scrambled to her feet and hugged the lyse fiercely before pushing him away. "What are you *doing* here?"

Before he could answer, a hawk swooped down just above their heads, crying triumphantly in the morning sky. The bird was Serena.

Suddenly something seemed quite clear. "Serena tracked us from the City," Linn said slowly. Thom nodded. "And when Faerin was taken by the eagle?"

Thom blushed. "Well, I am the master of birds, you know. Some birds still obey me. I sent a falcon to watch you first. Then the eagle. He rescued Faerin. I even sent the raven to the tree this morning."

Linn turned to watch Serena fly out over the lake. "Thom! It's not black anymore!" She turned back to him, arm outstretched. "Did you see that? It was black like molasses and now it's golden!"

Thom nodded, retreating to the line of grass above the shore. He began building a small fire. When it blazed hot, he drew Linn over and wrapped her in her bedroll. Then he made a mornmeal of fried tubers and onions with boiling tea. Linn ate until she thought she would burst.

Finally sated, the pair sat quietly watching the sun glance off the golden depths of the lake. Linn turned back to Thom and, with a stern look, said, "Come on. Tell."

Thom grinned a little, cupping his hands around his little metal mug. "All right." A sigh. "I couldn't bear it, Linn. I couldn't bear the thought of you all alone in the wilderness with only a baby kjaerdyr to protect you. So I sent Serena and a few other birds to trail you, and I trailed them. I was just half a day or so behind you. Sometimes closer."

Linn remembered her feeling of being watched and followed. The birds flying high above her had made her so apprehensive. . . . She started to laugh until she remembered Rane. He had followed her, too, so her fear hadn't been totally off the mark.

"But why? Why didn't you just come with me?"

"It was *your* test, not mine." Thom poked the fire

with a twig. "It was your chance to prove your path-finding gift. And you have to admit, you did prove it."

Linn nodded. Had it cost everything she wanted—for herself, her family, even Gee? She closed her eyes, savoring the moment when the Great One had taken her hand. His voice, his touch, his face filled her mind's eye, vivid and real—not something faked by Rane. "I'm so glad I breathed," she murmured.

Thom lifted one eyebrow but didn't ask any questions. Linn knew he was leaving what happened under the lake to her, to tell or not to tell. Like the test, that was private, for her alone.

The lyse cleared his throat and continued his story. "When I got here, I saw the lake, filled with that black liquid."

"It wasn't on fire?"

Thom shook his head. "Faerin was frantic! He ran down to the water, whimpering and barking at the lake. So I climbed the tree to see farther—just in time to catch you coming up through the water and paddling to the bank. As soon as you broke the surface, the water changed from black to gold."

He moved closer to Linn, refilling her metal cup with hot tea. He cleared his throat, pausing as if searching for words. "I did notice something else, Linnet," he said finally.

"What?"

"This." He took her wounded hand and turned it

palm upward. Where the angry red wound had gaped, now a silvery scar shone. A long, straight arrow.

Linn stared at her hand. It looked just like the other lysemarks she'd seen in the City. Maren's wheat, Liam's wheel, an eye, a paw print, a book, and many others. She flexed her hand, marveling that the pain, with her so long, had gone.

She looked up into Thom's face. Then, tracing the outline of the silver arrow in her palm, she asked, "Will you tell me now?"

"Tell you what?"

"Tell me what you said you'd tell me after my test was over. Remember? You were packing. And then the next morning you opened my palm and kissed my wound. Why did you do that?" Linn's eyes caught Thom's and held his gaze. And very, very slowly, the lysetett began between them, a tugging, steady heartbeat.

Just as slowly, Thom smiled. His eyes sparkled as, very carefully, he drew off his gloves, first the left and then the right. Then he slowly opened his right palm, revealing his own lysemark to her.

It was a long, silver crossbow.

ABOUT THE AUTHOR

By the time Aiden Beaverson was five years old, she knew that writing was going to be her life. Fantasies and science fiction books have always been her best friends. After earning a degree from the University of Wisconsin in comparative literature, she ran a bookstore, worked for a national nonprofit organization, and was a corporate writer and editor. A self-proclaimed animal fanatic, she now operates a freelance writing business in Madison, Wisconsin, where she lives with her husband, their two children, and her hedgehog, Tiggy. *The Hidden Arrow of Maether* is her first novel.